BOOK TWO IN THE #1 INTE
LIVING IN CI

C000145963

Tempt My HEART

JADE CHURCH

Content Warning

Tempt My Heart contains themes and content that some readers may find triggering, this includes but isn't limited to: *references to anxiety, alcohol use, references to drugs and suspected use, revenge porn, arson, violence/threat, death of a parent (past, off-page), stalking/harassment,* and *on-page sex and swearing,*

Also by Jade Church

Keep in touch!

Don't want to miss new release details, behind the scenes sneak peeks, cover reveals, sales, and more? Then sign up to my newsletter to get swoony romance updates straight to your inbox!

https://linktr.ee/jadechurchauthor

To you, the reader
xo

Tempt My
HEART

JADE CHURCH

Chapter One

You know what to do.

The words had been staring up at her for so long that she was starting to worry they might burn into the screen. Alison bit her lip as she glanced around conspicuously, eyes wandering more than once to the big glass wall that sat directly across from her desk. The blinds were open, sunlight cheerily pouring into the chic space, but it was the man grinning down at the phone as he spoke that really held her attention.

You know what to do.

The thing was, she *didn't*. Maybe for some people, the choice would have been obvious, easy. But Ali had never been very good at lying, least of all to herself... but, more importantly, never to her boss, Christopher.

He looked up at that instant and their eyes met, his smile slipping slightly before it hitched back up again and she looked down at her diary awkwardly, still seeing nothing but the words from the message on her phone.

1

See, she knew that lying to her boss and leading him on under false pretenses would never end well. Trying to score an invite to the biggest wedding of the year by being his plus one was never going to happen—regardless of what her ex threatened her with... or how she might feel about the boss in question. Not that there was anything like a Happily Ever After on the table for her and Christopher. There *was* no her and Christopher.

He was her boss. She was his assistant.

Could she be a bigger cliche?

In her defense, there weren't many men out there like Christopher Hanley. He was always unfalteringly polite, genuinely nice, and the way his slacks hugged his thighs was—Ali cleared her throat, willing the burning in her cheeks to calm down as she let the thought die a slow and miserable death. He was her *boss*. He might as well have had OFF-LIMITS stamped on his forehead.

So, she had to tell him. He deserved to know and, logically, she was probably going to save herself a lot of trouble down the road. But if she told him what she needed... If he couldn't help her...

Well, let's just say that she couldn't see her ex being the forgiving type if she couldn't deliver what he'd demanded. Given that she'd never expected him to be capable of blackmail in the first place, she couldn't predict what he would do to get ahead in his career as a journalist. Secretly filming your girlfriend (who you probably only decided to date because of her connections so you could capitalize on them) and then threatening her? Apparently, Jared didn't draw the line at any of that and it made her wonder what else she'd been too blind to see. Had he been overeager to come to company events? Had there been small bits of info she'd unwittingly leaked to him and the trashy magazine he often freelanced for?

She'd thought she'd gotten over her heartache for Jared already when he'd unexpectedly broken up with her via *text* while she'd been waiting for him at a restaurant in the city. Was there anything sadder than crying over breadsticks and a bottle of red wine in *Gino*'s? At least he hadn't papped her, she supposed. Not that anyone would be interested in her life—not unless it involved her boss. Not only did Christopher run one of the biggest interior design companies in the US, but he was friends with one of the most infamous couples in Cincinnati. David Blake and Rose DuLoe were the *it* couple of the moment, thanks in part to their ridiculous wealth and the various businesses they owned—but also because of the shock waves they'd made last year when a crazed-stalker had made an attempt on their lives.

Telling her boss what her ex was demanding would be mortifying, but what other choice did she have? Trying to trick or seduce him would only end in heartbreak and probably a job hunt after being rightfully fired.

Ali picked up the phone, teeth sinking into her bottom lip as she read and re-read the message before replying: *I need time.*

The reply came almost instantly. *Crap.* He must really want this to be practically sitting by the phone, waiting for her message. It was a short and to-the-point statement: *You have until Monday to decide.*

Ali glanced up at her computer screen and blew out a long breath. Monday. She could deal with that. Everything was going to be fine. She was going to figure this out. Everything was fine. It was all okay. It was—

"Ali?"

She looked up, pulled out of her spiral to see Christopher with his head sticking out of his wooden office door, and jumped a little as she met her boss' dark brown eyes. "Could you come here for a sec?"

Crap. He knew. How did he know? "Sure."

Clearing her throat lightly, Ali stood and smoothed down the waist of her pencil skirt as she made her way into the glass office. Christopher was already seated behind his desk and from anyone else, this would have intimidated her. As it was, she felt only a mild thrill as she looked up at him from beneath her lashes.

The thing was, Christopher wasn't *just* her boss. She'd been his personal assistant for about two years now and in that time they'd become... friends. It was one thing to lie to her boss, even if she was terrible at it, but it was a wholly different thing to lie to a friend.

"What do you need?"

He smiled at her and her pulse jumped in her throat. "I just need you to—"

Ali tuned him out. She didn't mean to, but it was hard to focus when she had other things on her mind. Like, for example, the ultimatum her bastard of an ex-boyfriend had saddled her with on what would have otherwise been a seriously nice Friday afternoon.

"Ali?"

She blinked, caught in Christopher's concerned gaze for a second before giving herself a mental shake. "Yes, sorry. Um, could you repeat all of that?"

His eyebrows furrowed as he watched her before he stood and came around the other side of his desk, leaning back against it as he ran his eyes over her face, probably not missing her pallor or the way she'd bitten her mouth nearly bloody. "Is everything okay?"

"Of course!" Her voice was too high, squeaky even, so she cleared her throat and repeated herself. "Of course. Everything's fine. Just Friday afternoon, you know?"

A small smile ghosted across his mouth and she found herself dazed for a moment before she forced herself to refocus. It was often like that between them—Christopher being innocuously gorgeous and her fighting to maintain the professional boundaries she needed if she was going to keep her cool. It was just hard when he was so damn *nice*. And single. Very, annoyingly, single. In fact, she couldn't remember the last time she'd seen him with a woman or had seen a date on his schedule. Of course, that made her imagination run wild—*clearly* her boss had shunned the advances of the women in Cincinnati in favor of gazing longingly at his assistant. *Ha.*

"Right. Well, why don't you take off early? We can discuss this on Monday. It's not urgent."

Her shoulders slumped as a relieved breath escaped her and she shook herself free of her thoughts. "Really?" It shouldn't have been surprising, he was a good boss. Attentive. Caring. He'd never once raised his voice at her —even when she'd accidentally spilled coffee over his undoubtedly expensive white shirt before an important meeting.

"Really." He smiled and she couldn't help but return it. "We've been working overtime this past week on the Clarence deal. You deserve a break."

How was she supposed to betray the trust and confidence of a guy that nice? Maybe if he was an asshole she'd be okay with screwing him over to save herself, but Christopher just wasn't that kind of person. She stood and smoothed her skirt again. "I appreciate it."

"Well, I appreciate you."

Heat flooded her cheeks but she pretended not to notice it, even as the slow smile on Christopher's face made her toes curl. She knew he was just being nice, supportive, despite her ridiculous fantasies. That's what made her stupid crush on him that much harder—knowing that Christopher was a genuinely good guy. Probably too good for her.

Her phone vibrated in her hand and she felt the blood drain out of her face. Was it Jared again? She darted a quick glance at it and let out a deep sigh when she saw it was only a message from her mom.

"You okay?"

She jumped, having forgotten she was standing frozen next to the chair in her boss' office. "Yeah, sorry. I'll see you Monday."

"Saturday," he corrected gently and she winced slightly before nodding—how could she have forgotten? He'd literally *just* mentioned the Clarence deal that the team would be celebrating on Saturday evening. It had been in the works for a long time and, as one of NYC's biggest office blocks and a prestigious brand to boot, it was a big deal that they'd landed this client. "Have a good afternoon, Ali."

"You too," she murmured softly as he moved past her to hold open his door, and she tried not to inhale the smooth scent of his aftershave. It turned out she had bigger problems than inappropriate feelings for her boss. Her ex, Jared, had made sure of that.

Her desk looked exactly as she'd left it. Organized to the point of being anal, the plant she'd been gifted by her mother on her first day two years ago was half dead, and her purse was tucked neatly under her dark office chair. She'd been Christopher's assistant the whole time she'd worked at *Horizons* and she loved her job. She was good at it. She wasn't about to let Jared take that away without a fight, but she wasn't really sure what her options were. Had she really not known him at all? Would he actually release the video of them having sex like he'd threatened? She just couldn't picture him doing something like this. Maybe it wasn't him at all, the texts had come from a blocked number.

Ali: How do I know this is real?

He hadn't sent her the video, just the threat, and she'd hate to do something rash for a threat that wasn't even credible. Surely if Jared had recorded them she would have noticed. Ali bit her lip as she tidied some errant papers.

Her desk was almost like an office—an open cubicle with filing cabinets under the side behind her and various in-trays on the section that sat to her right. The cut-off was three PM, but someone had obviously snuck in a few extra memos past the deadline while she'd been in Christopher's office. She rolled her eyes, but decided to let it slide this time as she sidestepped some crumpled paper and further into the space she'd carved out for herself.

Quickly tidying the notes on her desk and powering down her laptop, Ali froze when her phone buzzed again. He'd replied. The sound was amplified thanks to the hardwood it sat on and she felt as if it might make her teeth chatter. Dread pooled low in her stomach and she ignored the shaking of her hand as she picked up her cell and opened the message.

Fuck.

She shut the phone quickly, hand shaking as she closed her eyes and tried to take a deep breath.

When she felt like she wasn't going to pass out, she stood and tried to appear calm as she waved goodbye to Christopher.

Jared: Meet me outside.

Ali fumbled for her purse and snatched up her suit jacket, slipping it on quickly. She put one foot in front of the other, giving her boss one last measured nod through the glass walls of his office as she focused on getting the hell out of there, anxious to see if Jared really was the one who'd sent her the photo of herself or if someone had accessed his phone somehow.

The chatter in the office drifted around her as she made her way to the elevator and then out through the security barriers.

There. Standing off to the side and waving his phone in the air at her like this was all a joke and they were about to go out for coffee. Jared.

Her footsteps were a sharp march as she hurried over to him. What was she even supposed to say? Luckily, possibly anyway, he seemed ready to do most of the talking.

"Alison," he smiled at her and the chip she'd always found cute in his bottom tooth seemed to mock her. "I know this is probably coming as quite a shock."

Her throat was dry but she managed to squeeze the words out of her throat anyway. "A shock? What the hell kind of game are you playing? There's no way that video exists."

His hand wrapped around her arm and tugged so she would walk next to him down the sidewalk. "Oh Ali." He sighed, and for some reason the note of disappointment in his voice coupled with the sheer size of the hand gripping her made a chill skitter down her spine. But it was a ridiculous reaction. This was *Jared.* He wouldn't hurt her. "You're a smart girl. Let's not do this."

She bristled. *Smart girl.* She hadn't been a *girl* in quite a long time. She was nearly thirty and he was being a condescending asshole—one of his less redeeming qualities, honestly. "Do what, exactly?"

"I never wanted to hurt you," he said and despite everything, she wanted to roll her eyes at the flatness of his voice. "But you can do something for me, something I need."

"I really can't," she said, annoyed. "And I think we're

done here." She tried to tug her arm free and gasped when he pulled her closer, tightening his grip around her bicep. "Jared, you're hurting me."

He didn't let go. "I told you I didn't *want* to hurt you, not that I wouldn't," he said gently, like she was an animal that could spook at any moment. "The video is real, Alison." When she said nothing else, he sighed again like *she* was inconveniencing *him*. He tilted the screen on his phone toward her and her lunch curdled in her stomach as acid rose in her throat.

The back arching, the red hair swept off to the side, they were familiar. They were *her*. He'd recorded them without her knowing—had this been his plan all along? Date her to blackmail access to Christopher and gain access to the high-profile world he lived in?

"You planned this," she said woodenly, too shocked to do anything but stare at the video playing before she looked away, unable to take it anymore.

"I did what I had to." There wasn't an ounce of regret on his face, just a cold frankness that made her feel dizzy. "I need this story, Ali. Both for my career and the money, I'm not going to throw this opportunity away just because you were a nice lay. So now you know where we stand. You can have until Monday still, if you like." There was a smug tilt to his mouth that said the offer was hollow—he expected her to comply without question.

No. *No.* He didn't get to just do this to her and make her risk everything she'd worked for. The business world had grown a lot, but a video like this getting out would still be detrimental to her career, her reputation. Maybe if she were a guy, a sex tape wouldn't be a scandal—or at least it would blow over five-times faster. But it was hard to be taken seriously in the business world and this would only make her life harder, not to mention that this was a private moment and the violation alone made her heart quicken with anger.

She lunged for his phone and he snorted, surrendering it as he finally relinquished her arm. "Take it if you want. I have it backed up online. This isn't going away that easily, Ali." He left the phone in her numb fingers and stepped closer to murmur in her ear. "For what it's worth, the sex really was good. If I didn't need this so badly, maybe things would have worked out."

Jared chuckled as he moved out of her space, walking away as easily as he had a few months ago when he'd unceremoniously ended things without so much as a goodbye. He'd left the phone with her, the video of them still playing and she flinched as the sound of her own moans carried to her before she hit pause.

She'd been in a low place when she'd started dating Jared and, for a while, he'd made things better. Made her feel slightly less alone. Her dad had just died, she'd been vulnerable, and clearly this sick fuck had taken advantage of that.

A strange mixture of shame and anger swirled inside of her, clawing its way up her throat and making her eyes water until she hurried further down the sidewalk and vomited in the closest trash can. He'd seduced her and betrayed her and now he wanted her to do the same thing to Christopher. *And for what?* His career? *Money?* She shook her head, fighting the sting of tears in her eyes. The truth was that she hadn't even been worth a goodbye to him and she hated that it still *hurt*.

She wiped her mouth with the back of her hand and grimaced before walking away, just wanting to be back home where she could cry in privacy.

Jared may have got the upper hand on her before, but she wasn't about to go down quietly now.

Monday.

Ali had the whole weekend to work out how she was going to make Jared sorry he'd ever met her, and she'd be damned if she wasted a single second of it.

Chapter Two

S he was already drunk by the time Jesse and Freya found her at the apartment they shared, curled up on the sofa and crying as she watched *A Castle for Christmas*.

Jesse dangled her close-shaved head over the top of the sofa to peer at her, light blue eyes wide and framed by thick eyeliner. "Did somebody die?"

Ali shook her head and Freya gazed at her with concern as she sat down, lifting Ali's legs and plopping them onto her lap.

"Does somebody need to die?"

Jesse laughed throatily and the sound was almost enough to make Ali smile. Almost.

Tomorrow she would be okay. She would pick up all the stupid pieces of her naive heart and come up with a plan. But the moment she'd got home, she'd realized that tonight she just needed to cry.

"Jared," she managed to force out, and Jesse groaned.

"Again? I already told you, I can set you up with Tash from work and he'll treat you ten times better than Jared ever did."

Ali handed Jesse the phone Jared had left with her, and she looked at it with her brows raised before unlocking the screen and gasping. "Fucker."

"What?" Freya reached for the phone and Jesse handed it to her before standing and pacing up and down the room, cutting off Ali's view of Brooke Shields on the TV.

The jingle of the chains on Jesse's washed-out denim trousers was strangely comforting as Freya let out a slew of cusses as she locked the phone and set it on the squishy chair they used as a coffee table.

"Have you reported it yet? My father has a friend in the police department—we can get this scumbag arrested and—"

"No," Ali said, her voice sounding as scratchy as her throat felt.

"No?" Jesse crouched down so her face was close to Ali's before she pet her hair. "It's okay. You're right, you're probably tired from all the snotting you've been doing on the couch. We'll go tomorrow."

"No," she repeated and Jesse tweaked the septum ring poking out of her nose as if she couldn't fathom what the word meant.

"We're going to need some more information than that sweetie," Freya said, her green eyes gentle as she brushed her dark hair out of her face, leaving just her bangs to frame her high cheekbones and pointed chin.

"If I go to the cops, he'll release the full video. I don't want that out there, I don't want anyone else to see it and know how fucking stupid I am."

"What does he want?" Jesse asked, slumping down onto the floor and holding her knees just under the rips in her jeans as Freya grumbled a protest to Ali's words.

"He wants me to get Christopher to take me to Blake's wedding and then to leak photos of it to him."

"Why doesn't he just get a press pass?"

She looked to Freya and sighed, pulling her legs off her lap and tucking them beneath her. "Rose has insisted on no press at the wedding after everything that happened last year."

"Understandable," Freya said as Jesse snorted.

"She's a socialite, isn't she supposed to love the press?"

Freya shot her a sharp look and Jesse raised her hands in supplication. "I think you'd have a grudge with the press too if they falsely announced your death."

"Besides," Ali said as she sipped at the glass of water she'd had the foresight to leave next to her glass of rum and coke. "Rose is a businesswoman, not a socialite."

"So what are you going to do?" Freya said quietly as they all stared absently at the movie.

"I don't know. I have until Monday to figure something out."

"Well, we're here for you if you need us. Whatever we can do to help," Jesse said as Freya nodded and Ali scooched up so Jesse could sit on her other side.

"For now, I just need you to make sure I'm not drinking on my own."

"That, we definitely can do," Jesse said with a grin as she clambered over the back of the sofa to the kitchen just adjacent to their living area.

"Don't worry, Al. If Jared screws with you, he screws with all of us."

Ali smiled slightly before pressing a kiss to her friend's cheek. "Love you."

"We love you too, babe." Jesse grinned as she handed a glass to Freya and then sat back down. "But do we need to watch a holiday movie? It's barely spooky season."

Ali passed her the remote and she immediately put on her latest obsession—*Lockwood & Co.*

Freya wrinkled her nose. "What is this?"

"Ghosts'n' shit." Jesse didn't look away from the screen even when Ali laughed.

"This is, what, your third re-watch?"

"I'm a dedicated person," Jesse said with a shrug. "I swear if they don't renew it I'm going to riot."

"It's kind of like *Scooby Doo*," she explained and Freya looked back at her blankly. "Or like *Supernatural?*" Ali tried again and then shook her head when Freya still looked confused.

"Sometimes I forget why we're friends with you," she teased and Freya smirked.

"Well, that's easy. You're the smart one, Jesse's the sporty one and I'm the rich one."

"I'm not sporty," Jesse said, wrinkling her nose and Ali grimaced.

"And I'm not that smart." She nodded to the phone

where it lay after Freya had watched the video. "Case in point."

"Jared's a shitbag," Jesse said easily. "It could have happened to anyone."

Ali sighed. "Let's just focus on something else."

They fell quiet for a few minutes while they watched the screen until Jesse let loose a massive sigh that made it sound like she was about to burst.

"Okay but like, what's your plan?"

"Jesse," Freya scolded and Ali rolled her eyes.

"I don't have a plan."

"Maybe I should be your plan."

Ali raised an eyebrow and Jesse grinned, showing off the piercing under her top lip. "I can throw a decent punch."

Ali laughed, knowing that had been Jesse's intent. "We all know Freya's the scary one."

She gave a mock squawk of outrage. "How am I scary?"

"Tell us again about your cop friend," Jesse said, wiggling her eyebrows.

"You could totally get away with murder," Ali agreed. "Just rich people things."

Jesse cackled along with her and Freya pouted before giving in and laughing too. On the surface, the three of them seemed like an odd group of friends. But Ali had known Jesse and Freya since college, and they had reconnected by chance through her work with Christopher. He got to meet all sorts of people when it came to running the interior design company with his best friend, David Blake. Freya's father had been a client, owning a large block of offices in New York. Whereas Jesse was big in the art world and had designed some custom pieces for *Horizons* where Ali worked, putting all three of them back in touch. It was a small world, it seemed, but Ali was just glad to have them both in her life.

Freya suddenly straightened next to her and placed her feet on the edge of the chair-table. "Everyone in."

Jesse rolled her eyes but they both compiled, too used to Freya's impromptu photo shoots. Freya didn't work a regular job, but she could easily have afforded the apartment on her own—or, honestly, one a lot nicer, but she insisted she enjoyed their company. She spent the majority of her time traveling and blogging.

"All part of being friends with an influencer," Freya said with a flip of her hair and Ali chuckled. "We really should get an actual table at some point."

They all looked at the thick, fluffy brown block that they had their legs propped up on.

"I like the not-table." Jesse frowned and folded her arms.

"Me too," Ali chipped in. "It adds character."

Freya snorted but relented and they fell back into watching Lockwood taunt a ghost.

"One day," she said suddenly and both of her friends looked to her. "I just needed tonight to feel sorry for myself and wallow. Tomorrow I'll plan, okay?."

Jesse analyzed her face, twisting her mouth up on one side. "You have an idea?"

Ali smiled slowly and it felt a hundred percent real. "I'm going to call my mom."

Chapter Three

I t was funny how a good night's sleep could make you forget almost anything. Friday afternoon and Jared's threats felt distant under the morning haze of sleepiness, at least until her phone buzzed with a reminder.

Jared: Don't think too hard on it.

He'd attached a still from the video. The threat was clear, and as much as she wanted to just stay in bed all day, wallowing, she was also *pissed*. But what could she do, really? Short of breaking into his place and trying to delete the video from his cloud, which she wasn't sure she knew how to do, she was at a loss. It had been about two AM by the time she'd crawled into bed and even then she couldn't sleep, so she'd spent ages on her phone trying to work out what the law was in her state about blackmail and revenge porn. As best as she could understand it, she didn't have enough proof of the blackmail or threatening behavior, and it wouldn't count as revenge porn until Jared attempted to distribute it. She wasn't going to let him get that far.

Ali sighed as she cradled her phone against her white pillow case, squinting from the screen's glare against her scratchy, puffy eyes.

Her phone vibrated once in her palm before it began ringing, the chirpy tune making her temples throb in dissatisfaction after the alcohol-filled sob fest she'd held for herself last night.

"Hey, Mom."

"You didn't call me yesterday after work. Everything okay?"

She and her mom had always been close, more so after her dad died. They were all they had left. Usually Ali called at least once a week, normally after work on a Friday, but with everything that had happened yesterday it had completely slipped her mind. By the time she'd decided to call her, it was already too late for her mom to be awake.

"Sort of." She blew out a long breath. Her mom wasn't a traditionalist by any stretch of the imagination, and the term *free spirit* felt like it wasn't wild enough to describe her. As such, Ali knew there was nothing off-limits between them, no holds barred and no secrets.

"Jared messaged me."

"I hope you told him exactly where he could go."

Ali winced. "Not exactly."

"Alison Henderson. Do not tell me you got back together with this boy."

"No, nothing like that," she said quickly before rolling

over onto her back to stare up at one of the cracks in the corner of her ceiling. "I actually need your advice, and I need to get out of the house for a while. Can you meet me at *Lola's?*"

Silence on the other end of the phone. Normally Ali was begging for her mom to stay out of her life because she had a tendency to meddle, so she knew it had to be something big for Ali to actively want her opinion.

"Sure, kiddo. I can be there in an hour."

"Works for me. See you soon." She hung up and gazed up at the ceiling. Her mom lived just outside of the city in the rural neighborhood where Ali had grown up—in fact, she still lived in Ali's childhood home. *Lola's* wasn't too far for her to travel, it was mostly Saturday traffic that would slow things down getting into the main hub of the city, but the coffee there was worth the trip anyway. It was actually where she'd first met Jared. Of course, now she was wondering if he'd known it was one of her favorite places—just how premeditated had he been?

"Ugh." Ali flung her arm across her face and winced as she somehow tugged on a piece of her hair that had come loose from its braid.

She didn't want to lie to Christopher. Didn't want to betray him or make him complicit in her betrayal—and that was only if she could realistically get him to take any notice of her.

There was no way she could guarantee that her boss would take her to his best friend's wedding. Jared's plan had more flaws than she could count.

Freya: Are u awake yet

Jesse: NOBODY'S awake yet. It's FIVE AM.

Freya: If you're not awake then how did u reply?

Jesse: ...

Freya: @alihenderson I know u said not to bother but I spoke to my dad's cop friend. He said there's not much they can do until Jared releases the video.

Ali sighed, scrolling through the group chat to catch up on her messages as her mood plummeted further. It was already one in the afternoon. By the time she was just waking up Freya had apparently been on her morning run, spoken to the police on her behalf, and was now making pancakes judging by the smell wafting under Ali's door.

It was Freya's go-to hangover cure and Ali had to admit that she appreciated the forethought as her stomach growled loudly. One foot dropped out of her warm covers and then the other, but then the room rolled as she tried to sit up. Steadying herself, Ali tugged on her cozy PJ socks and shuffled into the kitchen.

Freya looked up with a smile as she dished pancakes out onto three different plates and slid one in Ali's direction.

"Heard you talking in your room. Your mom?"

Ali nodded as she grabbed the plate from the counter and carried it to the small dining table they had squished into the corner of the main living space. "Yeah, we're going to meet at *Lola's*."

"Well, eat something before you go. It'll make you feel more human."

She snorted but didn't disagree, wolfing down the hot

blueberry goodness before pecking Freya on the cheek and heading into the shower.

The hot water eased her throbbing head, and by the time she made it out the door she was desperate for a latte. The coffee shop was a short walk from her apartment, in a similar direction to her office, and it felt strange to be walking down the same street as yesterday and find it unchanged when everything else seemed like it was turning upside down.

Lola's had a sort of rustic coziness to it that immediately set her at ease, like a home away from home with its low-hanging lights, wooden decor, and woven rugs on the hardwood. Her mom had beat her there and claimed a small booth along the left wall opposite the counter, and the familiarity of her mom's smile and the scent of coffee beans made her finally relax.

"Hey." She smiled and slid into her seat with a sigh of relief before ordering a coffee using the app.

"How're things?" Ali knew her mom was probing but trying to be nonchalant about it, and she worked to hide her smile. They had a pretty relaxed relationship nowadays and she was grateful for it, especially when she slid her sunglasses off her face and her mom's blue eyes narrowed as she took in the slightly puffy, bloodshot remains of yesterday's crying. "I see."

"Mom—" Ali cut off her words to thank the waitress as she set down her coffee.

Her mom shook her head and the strawberry blonde of her hair practically quivered with rage. "Remind me where this boy lives?"

A laugh slipped out, unbidden, and she had to wonder if she was just hysterical at this point. If her mom was mad now... Well, everyone had better take cover for when she told her the rest of the story. She hiccuped slightly as the laugh threatened to turn into something else and she clenched her jaw to keep any more tears at bay. "I don't know what to do."

"Tell me," her mom said immediately, leaning forward across the table to take Ali's hand as she sipped her coffee with the other.

So Ali explained what Jared had sent her and what had happened when she'd met him outside the office, as well as his 'request' if she wanted to keep her sex life private and off of the porn sites.

"Fuck him," her mom said, predictably. "Let him release them," she followed up, this time taking Ali aback.

"What? No."

"There's absolutely no shame in sex, sweetie."

"I don't think he's bluffing." Though it was true that threats were one thing, actually following through was another.

"What do you have to lose?"

"My dignity? My professional reputation? I didn't know that he was recording us."

"Okay," she said, clearly understanding that Ali was never going to just let Jared leak the video or pictures of her. "What about the police?"

"Maybe," she murmured, taking a sip of her latte and melting at the rich flavor. "Freya did say she knew a guy.

But I'm just not sure what they would be able to do to help."

"Arrest him?"

Ali rolled her eyes. "I love your optimism. They said until Jared actually makes a move or I have more firm proof there's not much they can do."

"What about a restraining order?"

She'd considered that too while she'd been stressing out in the shower. "They take a while to get and keeping him away from me doesn't delete the video he has."

"Well." Her mom sighed as she drained her mug and reached for the muffin she'd ordered while Ali had been speaking. "You know the shitbag better than I do, sweetie. Do you think he'd go through with it? Could you talk him down?"

She wasn't sure why talking him down should be her responsibility—by all accounts it seemed like he'd dated her just long enough to get what he needed to blackmail her. "I think he planned this from the start." The thought was more than a little depressing. Sure, Jared was never going to be a forever-boyfriend, more of a grief-driven rebound, but she still hadn't expected him to violate her trust this way.

"You've got a tough choice to make."

"I know."

"Talking to him couldn't hurt."

"I'll try."

"You know I'm here if you need me."

Ali smiled. She did know. "Love you."

"I love you too, kiddo."

29

"How'd it go?" Freya asked as Ali walked in the door and kicked off her shoes.

"She told me to let him release the tapes and that there was nothing wrong with enjoying sex."

Freya snorted as she continued making her post-workout meal. "I don't know how we didn't see that response coming to be honest."

"I think I'm going to try and talk to Jared face-to-face again. I mean, the fact that his plan relies on Christopher taking me to the wedding already makes things impossible." Freya hummed in response and Ali looked at her sharply. "What?"

"Dude wants to bang you," said a gravelly voice from behind her and Ali jumped as she realized Jesse had come out of her room behind Ali's chair.

"What are you talking about?" She could only hope her face wasn't as red as she suspected it was. The smirk on Freya's face made it clear that hope was futile. "And did you only just wake up? That makes me feel better, to be honest."

"Are you forgetting that we came to that Christmas party with you last year? God, you two would have set the room on fire if you'd had any more chemistry."

Ali spluttered, the air getting stuck in her throat as she looked up at her friends with streaming eyes. "That's ridiculous," she finally managed after gulping some water that Jesse handed her. "Christopher and I—"

"There it is," Jesse said, nodding and Freya tried to

smother a grin. "*Ccchristopherrr*," she taunted. "Even the way you say his name is different."

Ali shrugged. "Sure, I may have noticed that he's attractive, but he's also my boss and just because I have a stupid crush doesn't mean those feelings are at all reciprocated."

"Oh, they are," Jesse said gleefully as she plopped down opposite Freya at the dining table and speared a cold blueberry pancake on the end of her fork before shoving it into her mouth.

Ali shook her head, unsure what else she could say, and Freya gave her a small smile—ever the peacemaker.

"I think what you really need is to not think about this anymore this weekend. You're going to give yourself a bad stomach."

It was true. Ali's body often reacted to stress with physical symptoms rather than emotional ones. "I'll be okay."

"I know, because you're coming with us to the spa tomorrow."

Ali raised an eyebrow as she looked between them. Things must have seemed dire for Jesse to agree to come to the *Sanctum*, the high-brow spa Freya had a membership pass for.

Typically, Jesse hated it—she insisted that the face masks gave her hives and the steam rooms were too hot and the massages were just uncomfortable. So Ali appreciated them both sticking by her—not that she'd expected anything less.

Ali sighed. "I don't know if even that will be able to

take my mind off of this. I just want to talk to Jared and get it over with."

"Give yourself some time," Freya said softly, standing up and wrapping an arm around Ali's shoulders before continuing to the kitchen and grabbing a glass of water. "He's not expecting to hear from you until Monday, right? So you should try and meet him then. Besides, you have that party tonight at *Horizons*—maybe you can test the waters with Christopher."

Ali shot her a sharp look. "There's nothing to test and, even if there was, I'm not going to just do whatever Jared wants. That means he wins."

"Monday makes sense," Jesse cut in and Ali released a slow breath as she tried to calm down. "It'll give you time to figure out what to say now that he's not springing this on you," Jesse added and Ali nodded slowly.

"Okay. Maybe you're right. I'll wait." What difference could a day and a half make, really?

Chapter Four

Polite applause scattered through the room as David and Christopher wrapped up their speech. It had been short and she knew everyone appreciated it. As well as a decent bonus, this party was their bosses way of saying thank you for their hard work and congratulating them on signing another big client. Normally Ali somewhat enjoyed these events—especially because it involved free food and usually good booze too. But it was difficult for her to relax and enjoy herself with everything going on, especially when it was all tied so closely to the two men who were now settling in on either side of her at the bar.

"The bar *is* open, right?" she teased, trying to keep her worry off her face and out of her voice as Christopher ordered a round. "So really we could have got our own drinks."

He raised a dark eyebrow at her as David laughed. "Sure, but first and foremost I'm a gentleman, Alison."

She snorted and his mouth softened, like he'd noticed she hadn't been herself since she'd arrived and was glad to see her laugh. Soft pop music played inside the bar *Horizons* had rented and she quickly looked away from him, worried he would see too much on her face. The bar was large and wrapped around one wall with plenty of seats running the length of it, but there was still more than enough room for people to dance or enjoy the buffet on the other side of the room. There was a real mix of people in attendance, some of whom had gone all out with their makeup and outfits and then others, like Ali, who had on her most professional but casual ensemble—dark jeans and a cute green sweater.

Even Christopher was slightly dressed down. It wasn't often she got the opportunity to see him out of the suits he wore to the office everyday but it haunted her whenever she did. There was nothing *casual* about the way Christopher's shirt clung to his biceps or the way his dark jeans molded to his thighs.

Ali took a hasty gulp of the drink her boss handed her and wrangled her thoughts back under control. It was hard to remember that he was her boss when his warmth suffused the space between them and she felt her shoulders relax, wanting to lean in closer.

"So you can be honest, Ali—whose speech was better?" Christopher rolled up his shirt sleeves and smirked at his best friend over the top of her head as she fought to keep her eyes off of the muscled forearms now on display.

David made a sound of protest as he signaled the

bartender for a glass of wine, his blue eyes sparkling as he brushed a piece of dark blonde hair out of his face. Ali raised her eyebrows at the still full glass in his hand and he grinned, nodding toward the doorway. Her bottom dropped out but she stopped her smile from falling as David continued to laugh with Christopher. "Hardly a fair judge, she's your assistant. Talk about *biased*."

"Ali is nothing if not fair," Christopher snarked and she remained silent as she watched the relatively tall, blonde woman David had indicated strut their way. "Plus, she's my friend and friends don't lie to one another."

Ali gulped, alcohol burning her throat as she nearly inhaled it. Rose DuLoe smiled at them before accepting the glass David handed to her. *Friends don't lie to one another.* Wasn't that what she was doing right that second? Acting like her ex boyfriend wasn't trying to breach the security Rose and David were trying to re-build for themselves and hiding things from Christopher in the process?

Her chest felt tight and her vision blurred until a hand settled over hers and squeezed before tugging her up out of her seat. She would have known that touch anywhere, so she let it guide her away from the bar and out into the lobby where the music sounded like a dull heartbeat reverberating through the walls.

Full lips. Wavy brown hair, free from the gel that usually kept the longer strands out of his face. Ali took in her boss warily as she leaned against the wall and sucked in the air like she'd been starved of it.

"Are you alright?"

It felt like her body was out of her control. She wanted to smile, to touch Christopher's arm and tell him that *of course* she was fine and definitely not considering an imminent betrayal of his trust and friendship.

Instead, her back slid down the wall until her ass hit the thin blue carpet. It was an odd choice for a bar lobby, she couldn't help thinking—clearly all that time working for a company that designed business interiors and office spaces was rubbing off on her.

Christopher sat down beside her and reclaimed her hand, propping it up on his knee as they stared at the gray wall opposite them.

"I didn't think my speech was *that* bad," he said and her lips twitched. "Ah, there you are. Do you want to tell me what's going on? You've seemed kind of out of it since Friday afternoon."

He was too damned perceptive for his own good. How could anyone expect her to trick this man? He was so much more than an admittedly-pretty face.

"Just a lot going on," she managed to murmur and he nodded slightly like he knew there was more that she wasn't saying but was being nice enough not to push her.

She turned her head and their gazes met and held. His breath was warm and smelled like champagne as it ghosted across her mouth. She hadn't realized how closely they'd been sitting until that moment, when her lips could have met his with barely any effort on her part.

So you're going to do to him what Jared did to you?

Ali looked away, sucking in another deep breath. No. She was better than Jared. She cared about Christopher, she didn't want to hurt him. How could she try and seduce him when she knew just how awful it felt to have that happen to you?

"You know you can tell me anything," Christopher said and then tilted his head, reconsidering, "except that Blake is more handsome than me. There are some things a man can't take, bruising his ego irreparably." Another weak laugh fell out of her mouth and he smiled like the sound was something precious. "Is it your mom?"

She shook her head. "No, she's fine. Honestly, there's nothing wrong. I don't know why I freaked out like that just then."

Christopher nodded, unconvinced. "Well, I'm here if you need to talk."

"Thank you," she whispered and when he gently tugged her down to rest her head on his shoulder she didn't resist, letting his scent wrap around her like it alone could protect her from all the decisions she had to make. She could easily have fallen asleep right then and there, but when the door to the bar swung open and a blast of music flooded out, she knew it wasn't right of her to take comfort in the arms of someone she might be destined to hurt. "I'm going to head out, if that's okay."

"Of course."

She smiled slightly and let him help her to her feet, both loving and hating the way her hair smelled faintly like his cologne, like he'd sunk into the essence of her.

"And Ali, if you need me... call."

She nodded, knowing that she wouldn't, and the tightness to her boss' jaw told her he knew it too.

Chapter Five

Her body felt like jelly.

"My legs are literally wobbling right now," Ali said with a snort. "It's clearly been too long since I had a massage that good."

"You know you can use my pass anytime you want," Freya said, raising a dark eyebrow at her and Ali smiled. "Pool?"

"Ugh, yes, finally," Jesse grumbled, stomping ahead of them in a way that was ridiculous considering the white flip-flops she was wearing, alongside a robe and swimsuit. The pool was probably the only part of the spa that Jesse liked—but for Ali, the massage was where it was at.

The smell of chlorine mixed with a floral, fruity scent as they walked in that made her take in a deep breath. Jasmine, maybe? The pool in the spa wasn't the kind you would do laps in—this one was round, surrounded by marble tiles with pink and beige veins. Water continuously flowed from hidden sockets in the walls, making a ripple of foam drift across the surface of the clear blue water.

They left their robes under a copse of trees that dropped fragrant blossoms onto the ground and into the water before they headed into the pool. It wasn't freezing but it wasn't hot either, perfect for dipping into after the steam rooms or the massage area.

Ali let her back rest against the cool tiled wall as she settled onto a seat carved into the edge of the pool. She'd remembered to tie her hair up this time—her red hair was volatile when provoked, and something about the pool water had made it go wild for almost an entire week the last time Freya had brought her. When she was younger, she'd often wished her hair wasn't so different from everyone else's. Less bright. Less intense. Eventually she'd fallen in love with it, even if seeing Jesse's close-shaved head did sometimes tempt her. She wasn't sure she could ever actually bear to cut it shorter than her shoulders.

Ali tilted her head back, letting loose a sigh as she inhaled the fragrant moisture in the air. "Thanks for doing this, Frey."

"Anything for my favorite people," she said, her bronzed skin still pleasantly flushed from the steam room, and Ali smiled slightly because she knew it was true. They all earned decent salaries, but they chose to live together because they enjoyed it. Jesse and Freya were her people, and she was theirs.

Soft chatter floated over to them as more people entered the pool area. Ali didn't look up, not until the voice fully registered, and then her eyes flew open as she whipped around to look.

Fuck.

She'd heard that voice a dozen times, smooth and elegant, the kind of femininity that felt sensual without appearing unprofessional. She'd never really spoken to her before, only seen her in passing at the office or work functions like the bar last night, but it was a voice that commanded attention in much the same way as the woman it was attached to.

Rose DuLoe. Otherwise known as Cincinnati's most eligible bachelorette, at least until semi-recently when she'd become engaged to David Blake... Christopher's best friend.

God. This was the last thing she needed right now. Another living, breathing reminder of everything she'd come here to escape—because the wedding in question Jared wanted her to leak details of? Rose's. And from everything Ali had seen in the press for the past year, Rose was not a person to mess with. After a stalker had targeted her last fall, the press and the cops had been next to useless, putting both Rose and David's lives at stake—the string of people Rose was actively suing was impressive to say the least.

Even makeup-free, Rose was gorgeous in a way that seemed out of reach. Though Ali supposed it was easier to look that good when you had an almost unlimited amount of money to work with.

A tall black woman walked by her side, her riot of dark

curls barely being restrained by an orange headscarf that made the rich hue of her skin seem to glow.

"Shit," Jesse muttered when she saw where Ali's gaze had gone. "Should we leave?"

It was true that the relaxation and calm she'd managed to find in the pool had washed away as quickly as it had settled in. "We don't have to—"

"I'm getting pruney anyway," Freya said, her full lips lifted in a soft smile and Ali again wondered how she'd got so lucky to have friends like these.

"I was ready to go as soon as we got here," Jesse quipped and they laughed as they waded out of the pool and over to their towels. They passed Rose and her friend with a smile and Ali tried not to groan when Rose called out a greeting to Freya, making them all halt and turn to see her.

"I thought that was you! How're things?" Rose's smile lit up her face and even Jesse looked a little dazed to be on the receiving end of it. "Have you met Maia? She works in design at *Horizons*."

"Oh!" Jesse exclaimed and Ali jumped. "I thought I recognised you. Jesse," she said, holding out a hand and shaking Maia's enthusiastically. "I've done a little work for *Horizons* myself."

"Jesse Cleaver?" the other woman crowed and Ali watched, bemused, as the two of them fangirled over each other.

"It's good to see you," Freya said, but her smile was polite—political almost. Most likely because Rose was a friend of Freya's family and things in her world could be... complicated. "I heard your dad's doing much better."

Rose's smile dimmed slightly and she blinked, her brown eyes becoming a little far away as she nodded. "Yeah, he's slowing down a little now and making more time for himself."

"Glad to hear it."

Ali had no idea what had happened to Rose's dad, and didn't want to draw attention to herself by asking. Besides, she could probably look it up and find the answer in the tabloids.

Jesse and Maia had just finished making plans for a dinner date and Ali was relieved to be leaving without having to exchange any words or pleasantries with Rose DuLoe until her voice called out sharply and Ali froze.

"What the *hell* is wrong with you!"

Oh god. Was Rose talking to her? How had she found out what Jared wanted Ali to do?

Ali turned and Freya cursed as a flash of light made her warm skin look pale.

"As if you haven't done enough!" Rose's voice was rich with anger even as it climbed in pitch. The woman at her side, Maia, looked more worried by the second, her hand settling on Rose's arm as a ripple of unease slid over their small group. Standing under the trees behind them was a woman clad in a towel and flip flops, wielding her phone like a weapon as she snapped several photos of them talking. Paparazzi. *Shit.*

How they had managed to get in the spa was anyone's guess, but Ali knew someone's head was going to roll for this. *Sanctum* had a strict policy about cell phones or any recording devices outside of the changing room. The fact that this woman had violated that rule, that *safety*, was a big deal for the high-profile members that frequented the supposedly-safe space. How could anyone relax knowing someone might be recording their most private moments?

Ali's stomach roiled as her own anger joined Rose's. Was the panic that now seemed to be tearing through Rose what Ali would soon be dealing with too? If she didn't help Jared and he released that video, causing a scandal for the company and for Christopher, would this be her life? Hounded by the press until she was as on edge as Rose clearly looked at that moment? Ali had never imagined that Rose could look anything except cool and collected, but there was true terror on her face that made Ali feel sick.

The fact that they thought they could do this, photograph them this way and invade their personal space further by hurling questions at the heir to the DuLoe empire while she was just trying to relax was beyond unacceptable. It was a shocking glimpse into what Rose must have been going through all her life, but more so since the attack on her and David and the media fervor since their wedding had been announced.

Any hesitation Ali might have felt was overrun by anger as the paparazzo woman dared to come closer, her black hair whipping Jesse in the face as she darted between the women to get the best shot possible of Rose. Maybe it was the way the woman knocked into Jesse and nearly sent

Freya sprawling, or maybe it was pent-up frustration towards a certain paparazzo in her own life, but Ali found herself gripping the dark-haired woman's shoulder tightly. The phone in the woman's grip was set to record and Ali's jaw clenched with disgust at the lengths these people would go to, the entitlement they must have felt to crash their way into people's lives like this. She snatched the device with her free hand and the photographer cried out in shock and maybe anger as she tried to wrangle it away from the death-grip Ali had on it. Ali elbowed her away and launched the phone out and into the pool.

Gasps sounded on all sides behind her but Ali didn't care, could only feel a smug satisfaction as she watched the phone sink beneath the surface. The paparazzo had gone limp, her face pale, and she didn't even resist as two burly security guards finally arrived and escorted her away with a hand on each of her arms.

"Ali," Freya gasped as she stumbled towards her and clamped onto her shoulders. "That was—"

"So badass," Jesse chipped in, the piercing under her lip glinting in the light as she grinned. "I almost wish I had that on camera." They shot her incredulous looks and her lips quirked up. "What? Too soon?"

Rose was shaking, though Ali never would have known it if not for the faint rippling of her blonde hair like she stood in a non-existent breeze. Maia wrapped an arm around her shoulders and that seemed to help. Ali turned away before Rose could try and say anything to her. She just wanted to leave. Sure, she'd taken down one paparazzo but she wasn't the hero here—not if she went along with Jared's plans.

Relief washed over her as Freya and Jesse steered her towards the exit without Rose calling them back to talk, or sympathize, or, even worse, thank her.

Anything she said to her would have felt like lies—how could you make small talk with someone you might have to screw over? Rose and Blake had been terrorized by the press enough last year, drawing a *lot* of attention to the company. Jared posed a danger to the reputation of *Horizons*, as well as to the couple's peace of mind. Unfortunately, the saying that all press was good press wasn't always accurate—especially when there are concerned members of the board breathing down your neck.

She knew she was imagining it, but the space between her shoulder blades itched as they walked away, almost like Rose's eyes were burning an accusatory hole there. Ali didn't look back. She could only hope that some remainder of the man she'd cared for remained deep down and she could persuade Jared to call off this madness. For all their sakes.

———

SHE'D BEEN on edge for the rest of the day. All the efforts of the spa session had been completely wasted on her, because she felt more tightly wound than ever. She hadn't heard a peep from Jared all day and it felt like she was waiting for the other shoe to drop.

Her phone lit up and she scrambled to check it, relaxing when she realized it was just an email with some kind of sale alert.

Biting her lip, Ali flicked onto the messages tab and stilled as she re-read her last text to her ex.

Ali: Meet me tomorrow. Need to talk.

She'd sent the message as soon as she'd got back from *Sanctum* and hadn't had a reply yet, but now there was a notification under her message—*read*. Motherfucker. Why hadn't he answered her?

She wasn't sure if she was making a mistake by asking to meet him face-to-face again. Maybe a small part of her still hoped this was all a bluff and their entire relationship hadn't been a lie, but she couldn't think of anything else to do but lay out the facts for him.

Fact one: Ali was a terrible liar. She stuttered, turned red, got sweaty, and was generally a disaster at it.

Fact two: Christopher was her friend and her boss. He had no romantic interest in her, and he wouldn't be susceptible to any 'seduction' Ali attempted. While he was her friend, she couldn't go to him with the truth, it wouldn't be fair to put him in that position.

Fact three... Actually, the first two had really covered everything. Jared's plan wouldn't work, even if she *wanted* to help him. Surely he couldn't refute the truth just because it was inconvenient? He *had* to listen to her.

With a groan, she decided to prod at him a little in the hopes of a response and an agreement. She just needed to look into his eyes now that she was actually prepared, and make her case.

Ali: Please, Jared?

This time he replied almost instantly and her stomach dropped at the still he'd sent from the video he'd been taunting her with. Her eyes were closed, her head thrown back and her hair was a red spill across his dark sheets.

Jared: Tomorrow. 8AM.

She exhaled a shaky breath before replying with a simple *thank you* and wanted to punch herself. Who thanked the person threatening them? *Someone who's trying to keep that person on their side*, she reasoned and felt slightly better.

What she really needed to do was some self-care. The spa had been a nice idea but seeing Rose harassed had reminded her of everything still at play and had undone any relaxation she'd been able to find.

She padded across the soft carpet in her room to the mirror on top of her drawers, reaching for the small silver jar in the basket next to it. This was her favorite face mask, and was one of the only luxuries she allowed herself—it was ungodly expensive for such a small jar. But Ali preferred to save her money for the house she dreamed of buying one day rather than splurging on temporary indulgences. Usually she was successful, but there was just something about this little pot of magic that she couldn't resist.

She massaged a small amount onto her face and neck after securing her hair into a messy bun on top of her head, and felt herself relax as she took in the cool sensation and the light chamomile scent.

Tomorrow was going to be a lot. She wouldn't let

herself think about what would happen if she couldn't convince Jared to see the truth—she would never be able to *seduce* Christopher. And not least because she'd never seduced anyone in her life. She took a calming breath and repeated the motion a few more times as the trembling in her hands threatened to overwhelm her entire frame.

Her mom had sent her several texts throughout the day and each one had made her smile. Some people might have found her overbearing, but Ali knew her mom only worried because she cared.

After twentyish minutes, she headed to the bathroom to wipe away the mask still left on her face, and paused on her way back out when she found Jesse and Freya waiting for her. Their faces wore almost identical expressions of pity and Ali sighed.

"It's going to be okay."

They nodded, unconvinced, before shuffling forward to wrap her in a hug so tight it was hard to breathe.

"No matter what, we'll be here okay?" Jesse mumbled and Ali felt warm at the words, knowing they would both move heaven and earth for her—and she would do the same for them.

"If you decide to murder Jared we'll help you hide the body," Freya affirmed and a laugh shook its way free from the cocoon of their arms before they let go.

"Noted." Ali smiled, surprisingly feeling a little better even if she knew it was only temporary. "I'm going to try and get some sleep."

They nodded and she blew them a quick kiss as she retreated into her room and climbed into the sheets. All she could do now was hope that tomorrow wasn't a complete disaster, and then deal with it if it was.

Maybe she was a fool to hope this could all go away with a civilized conversation, but it was all she had to cling to when the alternative was either having her privacy violated or having to betray Christopher's trust. Plus, having seen Rose's reaction at the spa, it was clear that the events of last fall had left a mark on her and likely David too.

Ali closed her eyes, and was still worrying when she managed to fall asleep.

Chapter Six

After a ridiculous amount of stress dreams, Ali was pretty sure she'd already experienced every worst-case scenario of the conversation she needed to have with Jared that morning.

If everything went wrong and Jared refused to listen, then she'd decided that the best thing to do would be to leave Christopher—and *Horizons*. She couldn't put the company through the explosive press that would result in someone so close to one of the CEOs having a scandal, nor could she put Christopher in a position to defend or condemn her. She would have to take the choice out of Jared's hands and resign if he refused to see reason. Sure, he could release the video anyway, but who would care by that point? He wouldn't be getting what he wanted and she could use some of her savings to travel abroad until the mess calmed down. At least, that was what she was telling herself.

She'd chosen her outfit with care for some reason,

maybe so she could resign with flair, or maybe to try and remind Jared of what she'd thought they'd shared.

Either way, the effect was impressive if Freya's expression had been anything to go off of when Ali had left her room in the close-fitting, but still office-appropriate, dress that made the most of her height and curves.

It was warm outside, even though they were now beginning to approach late fall, but she had slipped on a jacket for the brief walk to the office in the main hub of Cincy anyway. She'd met up with Jared hundreds of times when they were dating, so she wasn't sure why she felt so nervous, or why she kept jumping at every small sound. It was just Jared—but the problem was that she wasn't sure she'd ever really known who he was.

There was a slightly secluded spot around the side of the office building that would still give her a good view of the approach so she could intercept Jared, and she made her way to it as she glanced over her shoulder yet again.

Ali checked the time on her phone for what felt like the millionth time since she'd arrived and frowned when she saw eight AM had come and gone. She wasn't overly concerned though, Jared always had been terrible at being on time—usually because he got too wrapped up in whatever story he was working on.

A familiar silhouette strolled up the sidewalk like they didn't have a care in the world, and Ali tamped down a surprising rush of anger. Mostly she'd been worried and stressed about what Jared had demanded—it hadn't given her much time to focus on the anger she felt at his betrayal, so of course it was now all bubbling to the surface at the worst possible time. She needed a cool head for this. To be pleasant. Flirty, even. Two exes, meeting for a cordial chat.

"Jared!" Ali raised her hand and his expression didn't change as he altered his course to come up beside her.

"Alison." He wrinkled his nose as he ran his eyes up and down her outfit but didn't comment, bewildering her. Had he always disdained her and she just hadn't seen it? "I don't really see what we have to discuss. I've told you what I need. Have you made a decision?"

She tried for a smile and dropped it when it wobbled. "It's not going to work. Christopher doesn't look at me that way. He's my boss. Plus the wedding is only a couple of months away, they wouldn't be able to find a space for me and—" she continued to babble on and choked on her words when Jared's face remained impassive.

"You'll figure it out."

"What?" Her eyes flew wide and she bit back the urge to curse at him. "I won't just figure it out, what you're asking for isn't possible—"

"Make it possible, Ali. Unless you want a prime-time slot on the air."

"You wouldn't," she whispered and bit her lip when he smirked. "Was any of it real?"

"Sure." He shrugged and it blew her mind how much of his facade he'd let drop now that he'd got what he wanted. "If that makes you feel better."

Her temper flared and Ali nearly growled as she stepped closer to him.

"You bastard. What if I have you arrested, huh, what

then? You realize you're breaking a dozen laws with this little scheme? And for what?" She snorted derisively, trying to appear confident even if nothing she'd just said was quite true. "To show your tiny dick off to the world? To get a couple of pictures of a wedding?"

Any trace of civility on his face dropped, his brown eyes turning hard as his jaw clenched. "This story will make my career. Not to mention how much those pics will sell for."

Ali hummed, knowing she was treading a dangerous line but unable to stop her mouth from spouting more and more insults. "Oh yeah, I can see the headline now. *Pathetic pap jailed for revenge porn* has a nice ring to it. Or maybe *poor performance aired by prick pap.*"

"Bitch," he hissed, crowding into her space and Ali swallowed hard, half-wishing her mouth hadn't run away from her, as his hands grasped her arms bruisingly hard and he shoved her back against the side of the building. Her head hit the wall and caused a ringing in her ears, her stomach dropping as he leaned into her. "You'll do what I tell you to, Alison, or things are going to get a little uncomfortable for you" he said warningly, squeezing her tighter, his voice like silk as he sneered into her ear. She attempted to shrug him off, shaking her shoulders until he shoved her against the wall again, his face so close she could see the individual hairs in his eyebrows.

Her breath hitched and she opened her mouth without knowing if she would try to scream or beg. She never got the chance to find out as a shadow fell over them.

"If you like your hands attached to your body then I suggest you take them the fuck off of her."

Her eyes flew up as that voice dipped straight inside her and coiled tightly. A familiar pair of dark eyes, warm in a way that Jared's never had been, met hers briefly over Jared's shoulder before Christopher stepped closer.

"Don't make me repeat myself," he said quietly, his frame towering over Jared's as the menace in his voice raised the hair on her arms.

Jared released her, giving her boss an easy smile before he looked back at her unblinkingly as he backed away. "Remember what we talked about, Alison. You know, I've been missing your mom's cooking so if you have any more hesitations I can always go and pay her a visit."

Ice shot through her veins and she froze as he walked away. Maybe she could have lived with her own public humiliation if he'd released that video of them, but she wouldn't risk her mother. Ever.

"Ali?" She barely heard Christopher as he placed a hand on her back and steered her towards the front of the building and the entrance. "What just happened? Fuck, you're shaking."

The unexpected curse shook her out of her shock and she blinked at him. Usually unruffled, perpetually-calm Christopher was nowhere to be found. The intensity of his gaze made her feel like she needed to hide even as she reveled in it like a cat stretching in the sunlight.

"I'm okay," she managed at last, looking up at him in a daze. "I'm sorry about that, I didn't mean to put you in that position."

He raised a dark eyebrow. "I'm glad I was there. Can I get you anything?"

"I should be asking you that." She tried for a smile but his concern didn't lessen, the crinkles at the corners of his eyes staying in place as he assessed her. "I need to make a call and then I'll be straight up."

Christopher stepped back and she instantly missed the smell of his cologne as he cleared his throat and gave her a nod.

She turned away and pulled out her phone, hitting Freya's name and trying to keep her breathing steady as she waited for her to pick up. She needed to make sure her mom was safe, and Freya was the one with the resources to make that happen. Or, her dad was anyway.

Freya's voice filtered through to her and Ali relaxed slightly. "I need a favor."

Chapter Seven

S he knew Christopher was going to want more of an explanation than the brush-off she'd given him downstairs, given that he was her friend and not just her boss, but she still took a few minutes to compose herself in the restroom on her floor.

A mixture of emotions was rolling through her so hard she could barely keep up with them, let alone process it. Fear for herself, her mother. Anger at Jared for doing this to her and anger at herself for not recognizing him for the slimy bastard he clearly was—and a little embarrassment that Christopher had been the one to step in and rescue her.

She also couldn't stop the what-ifs swirling around her mind. If Christopher hadn't come when he had, what would Jared have done? Why had she let her anger speak for her?

She was lucky, was what it came down to. Clearly she had no real idea of who Jared was or what lengths he would or wouldn't go to, but the coldness of his pale face when he'd threatened her and then her mother had given her chills.

By the time she approached her desk she felt slightly more centered, if still lost about what to do from there. Her mom was safe, Freya had taken care of that, so at least it would only be Ali's reputation, career, and life that was on the line if she refused to do what Jared asked. She needed to talk to her boss, and leave probably the only job she'd truly loved, so that when the shit hit the fan it wouldn't blow back on him and the company too badly. She couldn't betray him, nor could she sit back and watch David and Rose be terrorized again.

And yet, she stayed in her seat, idly checking her emails as if her world wasn't about to implode. An hour passed. Two. Compartmentalizing had always been one of her strengths, but maybe this was taking things too far. Ali glanced up and found Christopher watching her through the glass walls of his office as he spoke to someone on the phone. Ali dropped her gaze, reaching for some files behind her and printing out a few documents that had just been emailed over to go inside the briefing file.

Once she was all caught up on weekend emails, she couldn't put things off any longer. But Christopher was still on the phone and she obviously couldn't interrupt... So with a heavy sigh, she opened up the software that recruitment used to headhunt talent and started to look for some suitable options for her replacement. It seemed like the least she could do.

After narrowing things down to what she felt were the

three strongest candidates, she hit print on the summation of their profiles she'd put together and then slowly stood.

Her heels made soft thuds against the floor as she made her way to Christopher's office and then paused as he swung the door open and stepped out.

"Oh, Ali. Are you alright?" His mouth was soft with concern and the olive tint to his skin seemed a little flushed as he straightened his silver tie.

"Y-Yes," she stuttered, caught off guard by his open gaze and the warm hand that steadied her elbow as she wobbled in her shoes. "I was actually coming to talk to you about—"

"Can it wait until tomorrow? I'm sorry, it's just I'm actually on my way out."

She blinked and then nodded, relief making her head feel light. "Yes, of course."

"Great." He smiled and she wondered, not for the first time, if he knew how stunning he was. "I've got an emergency meeting with Brickham, so I'll probably be out for the rest of the day."

Brickham. One of their more nitpicky clients they'd signed recently who owned a small, but rapidly growing tech empire. Once he got talking, you could be there for hours. "Of course. I'll redirect your calls and take messages."

"You're amazing," he said, flashing her that killer smile again and melting her into goo before he turned and walked away. Normally Ali could keep her head around attractive guys, but something about Christopher specifically undid her and she couldn't help imagining another circumstance where he'd tell her those words, his deep voice coasting along her skin, the warmth in his eyes a searing inferno as she ran her hands through his thick, dark hair...

Ali shook herself, realizing she was still standing in the same spot, rooted in place. She rolled her eyes at herself. Ridiculous. At least leaving *Horizons* would mean her stupid crush on her boss would fade. Or, she considered, tilting her head as she stared toward Christopher's empty office, he wouldn't be her boss anymore—so there was nothing holding her back from asking him out. Or maybe just a hook-up so things didn't get complicated.

A pang went through her at the thought of not seeing Christopher again and she pushed it aside, knowing that quitting was the right thing to do. She couldn't lie to him and make him betray his oldest friend and business partner, it wouldn't be fair and would undoubtedly just come back to bite her in the ass anyway.

Sitting back down at her desk, she looked out at the room around her, committing it to memory. Tomorrow she would be leaving here. Leaving Christopher.

Her phone buzzed with an incoming text and her mouth went dry at the photo on the screen. Jared was once again proving he would follow through, because on her screen was the view of her mother's house. There was the porch with the swing that was broken and the potted plant that had long since died. It would have seemed innocuous if not for his earlier threat. Her mind swam and tingles pin-pricked her fingers as she stared and stared at the photo before picking up her phone with numb hands and dialing.

"Hey kiddo, what's up? Aren't you at work today?"

"Mom," she said breathlessly, "I need you to listen to me closely."

There was a pause on the other end of the line and a rustle like she was putting down her paper to focus. "Okay."

"Jared threatened to hurt you if I didn't do what he demanded."

Her mom snorted. "Let that little weasel try. It's been a while since I shot anything."

"As much as that response thrills and alarms me equally," she said, beginning to relax at the familiar sound of her mom's voice, "Freya has someone there to help keep you safe. He should be outside the house in a dark car."

"I'm not sure that's necess—"

"Go outside and ask him to come into the house," she said, cutting her off. "Promise me you won't go anywhere without him, okay? His name is Caleb and Freya said he's one of the best."

"Okay, sweetie. If it will make you feel better."

Ali bit her lip and then decided to tell the truth. "Jared sent me a photo of the outside of the house."

Her mom didn't reply but she could hear the sounds of her moving, opening the door and then talking to Caleb. "You should have led with the fact that he's a gorgeous mountain of a man. I would have protested less."

A laugh slipped out and she relaxed fully, knowing a professional was there to make sure her mom was safe. "If I had known then I would have told you," she assured her, knowing her mom was probably just teasing. Her parents had been separated for a while before her dad passed, but it had still hit her mom hard.

"Check in with me every night, okay?"

"Yes, Mom," her mother teased and Ali chuckled, knowing she was maybe being a little overprotective. But she'd already lost one parent and she wasn't going to let Jared take the other from her. "I love you."

"I love you too," Ali murmured. "Stay safe."

"I will if you will."

It was such a *Mom* response that Ali smiled as she hung up. She had every intention of staying far, far away from Jared. Maybe she'd go to Paris, or somewhere with a beach and no cell service until things blew over or the wedding had passed. She could work all of that out later, for now she just needed to make it out of *Horizons* with her professional reputation intact.

Chapter Eight

If she believed in signs, then the universe didn't want her to quit her job. But then again, the universe had let her date Jared so what did it know, anyway?

She'd tried to enjoy a slow stroll into the office the next morning but had ended up practically running as her skin crawled with the sensation of eyes on her skin. Was Jared watching her? Or was he still camped out at her mom's? A couple of times she'd actually thought she'd caught a glimpse of him walking on the sidewalk opposite her but when she'd looked back it had just been another brunette, tall man. He was making her paranoid.

The elevator had been blissfully empty when she'd got to the office, and she was grateful because it gave her the chance to catch her breath after the intense pace she'd kept up on her walk.

That was where any semblance of good luck ended, however. The silver metal doors slid open with a ding and Ali walked past the rows of cubicles that held a few early risers before stopping dead in front of her desk around the corner.

How could she have forgotten that today was David's day in the office? Worse, not only was she unprepared to see his well-cut, blonde form in Christopher's office, he'd also brought Rose with him.

She swallowed hard and forced her feet to continue moving, rounding the desk and plopping down in her seat just as Christopher's door swung open.

"Ali," he said with a smile, and it felt like her heart stopped before resuming its pace at double the speed. He was wearing that light gray jacket that emphasized his shoulders and waist, she'd always had trouble focusing when he wore that suit. "I know you wanted to talk to me yesterday but I'm going for a brunch meeting with Blake and Rose. I can have a quick chat now before I go though?" he offered and she wrinkled her nose slightly as she noticed David and Rose hovering behind him. How could she resign with them watching? Especially if he pressed her and she ended up confessing—withholding the truth was just another form of lying and Ali was bad at that too.

"Oh, no. That's okay. You go and enjoy your brunch."

"Did you want to join us?" His dark eyes on hers were steady and warmth curled in the bottom of her stomach in response.

"I've got a lot to do," she murmured. If it wasn't for everything with Jared then she probably would have jumped at the chance to get to know the people in her boss' life a little better. As it was, she wasn't sure she could sit across from the happy couple without spilling everything she was keeping under lock and key. "But thank you."

"Maybe another time," he said easily and she nodded. He hesitated, staring at her for a moment in a way that brought heat to her cheeks before he nodded and turned back to David and Rose who were watching them with keen interest. "I should be back later, but if I'm not then don't work too late, okay?"

She laughed and the echo of it was still on her lips when she smiled. "Sure. I promise to leave at a reasonable time."

He waved goodbye and Rose smiled at her as she walked past to the elevators Ali had only recently vacated.

Ugh. Christopher was too charming for his own good and she wasn't quite sure what he was going to do when she told him she was leaving. She was a good employee and he was a great boss, so she hoped it would be alright. It almost felt like the buildup to getting to resign was going to be worse than actually leaving, but maybe it wouldn't be as awful as she imagined.

Her phone vibrated and she cursed as she saw Jared's name on the screen. He'd sent her at least four messages, each more threatening than the last as he waited to see what decision she would make.

Sometimes the photos were of her, others were her mom's place—both unnerved her. She wanted to protect the people she loved, as well as herself, but she wasn't sure what she should do. Maybe she could speak to an attorney or something and find out what kind of laws he was breaking.

Either way, if she wanted to keep everyone safe then she needed to do *something* to keep Jared out of her life.

"Hey, how'd it go?" Jesse called as she shut the front door and flung her purse into the corner of the room. "You're not drunk, so I figure that's a good sign."

Ali looked up and Jesse swore as she took in Ali's puffy eyes ringed in red and the blotchy state of her skin.

"I'll kill him." Jesse spun towards the door as if she was going to do just that when Ali patted the space next to her on the couch.

"It's okay," she said, voice thick from the sobs that had wracked her body as soon as she'd got home and found Jared waiting on her doorstep. He hadn't said anything to her, just smiled in a way that made her queasy. He had nothing left to say to her until she made a decision, so she could only assume his presence had been a threat—a reminder that he knew where she lived and what her routine was. "Today was just... It sucked."

"What happened?"

She shrugged. "He was waiting outside of the apartment building."

"Bastard." Jesse's nostrils flared and it soothed something inside that her friend was so pissed on her behalf. "Then what happened?"

"He just left, not like last time when he grabbed me and—" *Crap*. She'd deliberately not mentioned her previous encounter to her friends, mostly because she hadn't seen much of them at home the past couple of days. It was easier to keep the truth to herself when she didn't have to see them.

Jesse's eyes flashed as she frowned at Ali. "And?"

"Christopher showed up and told him to take his hands off me."

Jesse's mouth fell open before her eyes lit up, a smirk crossing her mouth. "I knew I liked him."

Ali snorted. "If I hadn't been so scared, it would have been funny. I think his exact words were something like, *if you like your hands attached to your body then I would recommend letting her go.*"

Jesse cackled and Ali couldn't help but laugh too.

"Is your mom okay? Are you? I can't believe you didn't tell us what happened."

She winced. "I'm sorry. My mom's fine, I asked Freya to send a guy over. I'll be fine too." For the most part, she was just having trouble reconciling that any of this was actually happening to her or that she'd let herself be taken in by Jared. "I just feel like an idiot to have let him put me in this position."

"You couldn't have known," Jesse murmured and she knew she was right.

"I guess." Ali sighed. "Anyway, enough about me. What's up with you?"

"Me? What makes you think something's wrong with me?"

Ali ran an eye over Jesse's make-up, noting the bright red lipstick, and the fresh piercing at the top of one of her ears. "You only wear red when you're mad and you only get new piercings when you want to cheer yourself up."

"You know me too well." Jesse wrinkled her nose. "It's nothing really. I slept with someone the other night and they didn't call me back is all."

"I'm sorry. But if they can't see how amazing you are then it's their loss."

Jesse half-smiled and patted her on the leg. "I'll get over it. Is Freya out tonight?"

She nodded. "Seeing her dad I think."

"Wanna watch a movie?"

"Sure," Ali said as she stood. "I'm just going to wash some of the tears off my face first."

Jesse smiled. "You've cried it all out now, babe. Don't waste any more on that asswipe. You'll get dehydrated."

Ali laughed and silently agreed, even if her tears had been more for herself than Jared and borne out of stress and frustration. Tomorrow was a new day, she wasn't going to let anything ruin it. Not even her pending resignation. She was doing the right thing, even if it hurt. There would be other jobs.

There won't be other Christophers, a sly voice inside her countered and she shook her head, deciding to ignore it.

Leaving *Horizons* would be a clean break for both her head and her heart.

Chapter Nine

She never normally felt nervous standing in her boss' office. It was a more recent development, thanks to her ex and the secrets she'd been keeping.

Christopher sat behind his desk, watching her, and the weight of his brown eyes on her skin only heightened the nerves pulsing through her body as he gestured for her to sit in the seat opposite him.

"I'm sorry I've been so busy the past couple of days. What's on your mind? Is this about what happened with your boyfriend the other day?" There was something assessing in his gaze as he spoke, like he was testing her somehow and she raised her eyebrows in response.

"Ex. And not really, no." She paused, wrinkling her nose. "How did you know Jared was my boyfriend?"

He leaned back into his chair, his suit jacket falling open as he watched her. "I notice a lot of things about you, Ali."

She swallowed, suddenly feeling like her tongue was

too big for her mouth. "Oh. Right. Well, I actually wanted to tell you I'm resigning and to give you these." She held out the papers she'd printed with details of potential replacements and he didn't even glance down at them, instead keeping his gaze focused solely on her.

"I'm confused. Where is this coming from?"

"I just need a change," she said dismissively, despite the heartbeat thundering in her chest. She'd never been a good liar, but she didn't want to involve him in this mess any more than he was already. "I've loved working for you, though."

"Are you unhappy here?"

"Well, no—"

"Do you need a raise?"

"My pay is fine—"

"Then why don't you tell me what's really going on here, Alison?"

Christopher stood and walked around his desk, leaning back against it as she gulped.

"I don't know what you want me to say."

"The truth. You're a horrible liar and we both know it. Your face is almost as red as Cassie's blouse right now," he said, nodding out of the window as Cassie strolled by clad in maroon. "If this is about yesterday, with Jacob—"

"Jared," she corrected and his eyes flashed.

"Right. You don't need to worry about him, I'll have him kept off of the premises."

She sighed. "We're friends, right? I've known you for two years, I introduced you to *Arthur's* burgers and, unfortunately for us both, I've seen you puke up a lot of sake." Christopher nodded, grimacing slightly at the mention of the Japanese wine, so she continued, "Then trust me when I say this is for the best. I made some suggestions for replacements—"

"I don't want a replacement," he said, folding his arms across his chest like she was the one being unreasonable. "I just want *you*."

Fuck. Ali could feel the heat rising in her cheeks once more, even though he hadn't meant it *that* way. She hadn't wanted to get into this, but if it was the only way he would see sense...

"He wants me to seduce you," she blurted and wanted to crawl under a rock when Christopher sat up straight, lips twitching.

"Oh? Then you should know my favorite color is green and I like it when my women are bossy in the bedroom."

She crossed and uncrossed her legs, trying to shake the image of Christopher in bed out of her mind. "I didn't agree to it, obviously. You're my boss."

He raised a dark eyebrow. "Continue."

One of her fingers tugged idly at her hair and stilled only when he reached out with one hand to gently untangle the red lock. "He's a journalist. He wanted me to be your plus-one to David's wedding and leak the details so he gets the scoop, seeing as it's a press blackout."

"Interesting," he said slowly and she bit her lip. "Seems like extraordinary lengths just for a wedding. I take it you turned him down?"

She nodded hesitantly. "The photos will be worth a lot

of money and he seems to think that an exclusive scoop will make his career."

She watched as Christopher made a small hum of acknowledgement before standing and paced the room. "So why does that mean you have to leave? I'm missing something."

She cleared her throat. "He has... a video. Of me. Me and him."

Christopher froze with his back to her and his shoulders tensed before he turned around and nodded like what she'd said was no big deal. A flicker of irritation made her grit her teeth but she pushed it down.

"So it's not a good idea if I still work here when he releases it." Ali stood to leave, figuring that was that and he would let her go. Instead, his next words stopped her cold.

"Tell him you'll do it."

Her mouth dropped open and she could only stare at him for a few seconds before his words registered. "Do what?"

"Let's buy some time," Christopher said, like it was the most logical thing in the world. "I don't want to lose you— as an assistant," he said, almost like an afterthought, "so tell him you'll do it."

"And then what?" she snapped, annoyed he was ruining all of her carefully laid plans, her sacrifice, on a suggestion that would go nowhere. "What do I do when he wants me to send him things? Photos? Are you really okay with screwing over David?"

He walked closer to her, steadying her with his hands on her shoulders. "If it comes down to it, then I'll do what I have to do. But I think we can stop him before it gets to that point. Not all hope's lost yet, Ali. Maybe I can talk to Blake."

"You don't need to do that for me, it's not worth risking your friendship just for an assistant."

"You're not *just* anything, Ali." He scrubbed a hand over the stubble on his face and then nodded, resting his eyes on the phone on his desk. "He's my oldest friend. I'll talk to him and then we'll go from there, but I think I need to do it in person. It doesn't seem like the kind of conversation we should have on the phone. Okay?"

For a second they just seemed to stand there, breathing in each other's air, until she let her shoulders slump and nodded. "Fine. But if this doesn't work... Well, what exactly are you suggesting we do?"

"He wants you to seduce me, right?" She nodded and he continued. "Then seduce me. Let him think his plan is working."

She swallowed. "Meanwhile you'll talk to David?"

"Yes. Plus, I also have a friend who might be able to help us get rid of that video so Jason doesn't have anything on you."

"Jared," she corrected and then bit her lip. "He said he'd hurt my mom," she whispered before adding, "and me."

Christopher's jaw hardened as he cupped her face with one hand, peering down closely at her as if to ensure that she believed his next words. "Jackson will have to get through me first."

"Jared," she murmured absently, too dazed by his

proximity to do anything else, and Christopher nodded slightly.

"That's what I said."

Her lips twitched but her amusement quickly faded as she considered what he was offering her. "You don't have to do this. I can just leave, disappear for a while."

His grip tightened on her face for a second before he let her go and took a step back. "Don't be ridiculous. Do you know how hard it is to train a new assistant?"

She rolled her eyes but smiled. "Thank you. For helping me."

"Of course," he said softly. "But don't expect preferential treatment just because you're sleeping with the boss." He smirked and she tried to ignore the way the words made her stomach swoop and fill with butterflies. God, she was in big trouble. Dating the boss. However she was expecting this meeting, or in fact her day, to go, it wasn't with the expectation that she would be walking out as Christopher's girlfriend. Even if it was only pretend.

"I hope we know what we're doing," she muttered quietly to herself and jumped a little when he responded.

"You and me both."

She left his office feeling strangely buoyed and had to sternly chastise herself. Regardless of her crush, she had to remember this was only a business arrangement. A ruse to save her skin that Christopher had been generous enough to suggest—and that only made it harder to keep her thoughts professional.

She picked up her phone and opened up her message thread with Jared before glancing one more time in the direction of Christopher's office. He was already watching her. He looked at the phone in her hand meaningfully and nodded, like he'd known she would need one last confirmation before she did this.

Alison: I'll do it. Just leave my mom alone.

Jared: Good choice.

It was done. There was no going back now.

Ali felt her tension fading as her adrenaline finally settled. She'd walked into that office intending for this to be her final day at *Horizons*—instead she was working with her boss to take down her ex.

Her phone buzzed with a text from Christopher and she felt oddly nervous as she opened it.

Christopher: I lied before, by the way. My favorite color is red.

Chapter Ten

S he looked between Jesse and Freya's faces
anxiously as they stared at her, both lost for words
for once as she sipped on her rum and coke.

"You were going to quit?" Freya demanded at the same
time that Jesse exclaimed.

"I knew you liked him!"

"He's not going to actually be my boyfriend," she
reminded Jesse gently and then raised an eyebrow at
Freya. "And yes. I wasn't going to give in to that asshole."

"So now you're playing him but he thinks that he's
playing you?"

Jesse squinted, mouthing Freya's words as if struggling
to make sense of them. It probably didn't help that they
were three drinks in at one of their favorite cocktail bars in
the city. "This seems overly complicated. Are you sleeping
with your boss or not?"

"Not," Ali said firmly and her friends gave each other a
look that made her frown. "*Not*," she repeated, pouting.

"Yet," Jesse said with a grin as she unfolded herself gracefully from the table and wandered over to the bar to grab another drink, calling behind her as she went. "No point living in denial, babe."

"I'm not living in denial!" she spluttered and Freya winced. "You're missing the point," she said, taking a deep breath and blowing it out quickly. "It's over. Christopher's friend is going to get the video back and then he'll have nothing to blackmail me with."

"And in the meantime...?" Jesse prompted as she sat back down a few minutes later with a long island and a bowl of chips.

Ali grit her teeth and bit out, "In the meantime I'll be pretending to seduce Christopher, and he's going to talk to David and Rose."

"Christopher. Your boss," Jesse added, as if she needed reminding. "And how exactly are you going to *seduce* him? How are you going to sell it? Make it believable?"

Ali paused. It was possible that she'd been so relieved she hadn't really considered the exact ramifications of this deal. "I—Well, we'll figure it out. If Blake can help then we might not need to keep up this ruse in the first place."

"Are you going to let him kiss you?"

She shot a look at Freya for joining in with Jesse's questioning, even as her face flushed. "What? No! Of course not. Why would I?"

"I think a seduction usually involves some touchy-feely stuff," Jesse said with a shrug. "You should wear that dress tomorrow—the one that makes your boobs nearly fall out the front."

Ali gaped at her. "I threw that out months ago."

"And I rescued it for you."

Sometimes Jesse's tendencies to meddle were endearing, other times they just left Ali speechless. "Why?"

"There was nothing wrong with it."

"It doesn't fit," she said with a sniff and Jesse shrugged liked *she* was the one being unreasonable.

"I think what Jesse's trying to say is that you might need to step up your wardrobe game to appear suitably... distracting."

"You're not slutty enough," Jesse said immediately afterwards, and a pinched look fell across Freya's face. "What? Being a little slutty isn't a bad thing. You should set some ground rules for him."

"Like what?" Ali said slowly and Jesse sat up straight, a brightness entering her eyes that nearly looked feverish.

"You know, simple stuff. Kissing's okay, but no tongue. He can touch your boobs, but only above clothes.That kind of thing."

Now Freya was the one staring at Jesse like she'd lost her mind. "Why do you know so much about this?"

"You're telling me you've never pretended to date someone before?"

"No," they said in tandem and Jesse blinked before looking away and out toward the crowded room as if she needed to collect herself. It had been relatively quiet when they'd first arrived but now the small tables and larger booths were almost all full and the golden lighting made everything feel warm and cozy.

"Why would we...? You know what, never mind. Look, I'll figure this out. I'm sure we won't even get to that point. Christopher's friend will track down Jared or whatever it is he's going to do, or maybe David can help, and then everything will go back to normal."

"I admire your optimism. It's sweet, really," Jesse said, squinting at her like she was a fascinating bug under a microscope.

"I think there's no harm in setting some boundaries," Freya said, glancing at her to measure her reaction before directing her gaze back to her phone as she edited a photo for her socials. "You're both friendly, right? So what's the harm in a frank conversation?"

Ali hummed in acknowledgement. It was true that they were friends—they'd been forever bonded after a memorable meeting with a Japanese client where Christopher had become hideously drunk on sake. He didn't typically drink but there were certain customs that this client appreciated when it came to his business partners, and Christopher had wanted desperately to impress them. It had been possibly one of the messiest work days she'd ever had, but also one of the funniest. He had spent the longest thirty minutes of her life trying to adequately describe the 'living fire' that was her hair.

Who knew the ever-charming Christopher Hanley could be such a poet?

"I'll talk to him," Ali decided and Freya looked relieved as she gently set down her phone and inspected her nails. They were perfect, as always, and Ali knew Freya would most likely touch them up later to ensure they stayed chip-free. It always seemed funny to Ali that Freya liked to do them herself rather than visiting a salon but she'd always claimed she found the process soothing—and in all honesty she'd become so well practiced at it that her nails looked stunning regardless. Ali often let Freya do hers too.

"And you'll let me dress you." Jesse smirked and Ali groaned.

"No."

"Please?" Jesse batted her lashes and widened her blue eyes with a pout and Ali sighed.

"You can advise. That's it."

"Deal." Jesse's smile was full of mischief and Ali already regretted the decision to let her have any part in dressing her tomorrow for work.

Chapter Eleven

"A re you sure you want me to come with you?" she asked anxiously as Christopher held open his car door. They'd left in the middle of the workday, and they'd left *together*—maybe it wouldn't have seemed so conspicuous to the rest of the people working on their floor if not for the arm her boss had kept around her waist as they'd strolled past to the elevator.

Yes, they needed to sell this ruse so that Jared got wind that she was doing as she was told. But the stares and whispers... Well, Ali wasn't used to being the subject of gossip around the office or otherwise.

"I just think maybe it would be better if it was just the two of you alone," she tried again as he walked around and climbed into the driver's side.

"I want you to be there," he said simply and she sighed with a nod.

"If that's what you think is best."

They fell silent for a minute as Christopher pulled his

car out of the lot and drove out onto the street. Rush hour had ended, but it was still busy as they headed for the road that would take them to David Blake's manor house on the outskirts of town.

"I got in touch with my friend," he said unexpectedly, and she turned from looking out of her window to watch him as he talked. "He's going to come to the office tomorrow if things don't go well with Blake."

She nodded. "Thank you." The drive was smooth and she was weirdly turned on by the ease with which he controlled the vehicle, his hands steady on the wheel and his body relaxed against the leather seats. "Why do you call him that? Blake?" she asked to distract herself from the annoying turn her thoughts had taken.

Christopher blinked, shooting her a quick look before he re-focused on the road. "I don't know. To be honest, it's just what I've always called him. We grew up together, you know." She did. They'd also gone to the same college. "I think it was just this unspoken *thing* that only his mom called him David."

Ali smiled slightly. It was hard to picture the powerhouse that was David Blake as a boy rebelling against his parents by shunning his name. Especially when that name was as prestigious as his—the Blake family had almost as much wealth as the DuLoes, a legacy around Cincinnati. Together, they were an impressive couple.

A shrill alarm sounded behind them and Christopher swore, his hands tightening on the wheel. "There's no way they're flashing their lights for us, right?" He glanced into the rearview and cursed again as the officer in the car behind them flagged them down.

They slowed to a stop, and Christopher tapped his hands on the steering wheel impatiently as the officer ambled over with almost deliberate slowness.

"Hi officer," he said pleasantly after rolling down his window. "Can I ask why you've stopped me?"

The man grunted, his small eyes squinting inside the car as he kept a hand on his belt by his radio and gun. "Got a report that this vehicle is stolen."

Christopher snorted. "That's ridiculous. This is my car."

The officer nodded like he'd expected that response. "Right. Can I see your license and registration?"

"Sure," Christopher said with a roll of his eyes. "Anything else?" he said, somewhat sarcastically as he reached for the compartment in front of the passenger seat and the cop's nostrils flared.

"I'd like to take a look inside the vehicle."

"I'm sure you would."

Ali tensed as the two men glared at each other before Christopher shut the door with a tight jaw. "It's not in here."

"What a coincidence," the officer sneered before peering in the back seat and walking around to the back of the car, waving for Christopher to pop the trunk.

"Doesn't he need a warrant for that?" she hissed and Christopher shrugged.

"Not if he thinks he has probable cause that the car is

stolen. Honestly, whatever gets us back on the road the quickest."

It was clear that he thought this was just some kind of ego trip for the cop who had walked to the back of the car, but she had a bad feeling about this. What were the chances that they had been stopped by the police while on their way to confess to David what her ex's plans were?

"Sir, if you could step out of the vehicle."

"What?" Christopher's eyebrows furrowed but he undid his seat belt and got out to check the back, his eyes flying wide. "No. I don't know how that got there but it isn't mine."

Fuck. She'd known something had felt off about this. Ali scrambled out of the car but kept well away from the cop, lest he think she was attempting to intervene.

"Let's continue this down at the station," the cop said and the wide surprise of Christopher's eyes as the cop thrust him against the side of the car and cuffed him made it clear that he was in too much shock to even consider resisting. "There's enough there for intent to distribute."

This couldn't be right. Everything she knew about police procedurals was from the TV but the way he'd grabbed Christopher, had been suspicious from the off-set... it was like he'd been *looking* for a reason to arrest him. And who had reported the car as stolen anyway? Too many things weren't adding up.

She peeked around the corner of the trunk and her mouth dropped open. Inside were bags of snowy white powder—lots of them.

"Ali," Christopher called as the cop tried to cart him

off. "My phone," he said, nodding to the seat, "call Wayde. Tell him what happened."

"Okay," she said faintly as the cop secured Christopher in the back seat and then came back in her direction to photograph whatever was in the trunk and call it in.

Nothing about this felt right and Ali bit her lip. Surely this hadn't been Jared's doing? She wasn't even sure how he would know how to get a hold of that much cocaine, but it certainly shed some light on his sudden need for money if this was the stuff he was mixed up in.

"Sorry ma'am, we're going to be impounding the car and I'd appreciate it if you would come with us to the station."

Her palms started to sweat and she had to swallow twice before she could speak. "Am I under arrest?"

He considered her, tilting his head to the side as his face stayed blank. "What's your relationship to the driver?"

"H-He's my boss," she said after only a slight moment of hesitation.

The cop nodded, the flat blue of his eyes creeping her out as he gestured her towards the squad car. "You're not under arrest, but I would appreciate you coming to the station to answer some questions."

Relief made her eyes swim for a moment before she blinked the moisture away. "Sure." This was getting out of hand. Reporting the car as stolen and planting drugs inside was too far. There was no way the police could ignore this.

She climbed into the front seat and jumped when the

officer's radio blasted out a confirmation that a team was coming to collect the car. It felt oddly stuffy inside despite the cool air outside and Ali wrinkled her nose when the officer shut the door, making the space feel even more enclosed as he started the engine.

"It's going to be okay," Christopher said quietly from the back as they moved off and she nodded, swallowing an inappropriately timed laugh that he was comforting her even though he was the one cuffed. "Call Wayde."

She did as he asked and left a voicemail explaining where they were going and what had happened. One thing was clear—her boss had been set up.

Her lap vibrated and she glanced down, assuming Christopher's lawyer was attempting to call them back. Instead, her own screen was lit up with Jared's name displayed prominently.

"Hello?" she said cautiously and grimaced at the heavy breathing that came through over the line. "What do you want?"

"I want you to hold up your end of the deal. Did you think I wouldn't be watching? Or that I'm stupid? You should probably be a little more aware of your surroundings before you go gossiping with Freya and Jesse over cocktails."

Ali opened her mouth to reply and snapped it closed when he cut her off.

"Tell me this was a mistake and that you'll do what I've asked, and I'll let my cop friends know this was all a misunderstanding."

Fuck. Jared had friends on the force? Well, she

supposed it made sense for journalists to have contacts at the department but this... She'd never expected this.

"You've got it wrong," she said, trying to keep her voice even as she glanced back at Chrsitopher and found him watching her, a line of worry burrowing into the bridge of his nose. "We were just—"

"Going to tell your boss' bestie that someone's targeting them so that they can either beef up security for the wedding or worse, let everybody in. How will I get my exclusive then, Alison?" His voice held a hysterical note that made her cringe. He was losing it, of that she was certain. "So promise me, right here right now, that you're going to behave. Otherwise your boss will find himself in a very sticky situation. And who knows, maybe you've been helping him with his little operation? What kind of assistant *are* you Ali?"

"If this is about money—"

Jared's laugh sounded ragged. "It's about so much more than that. Money, legacy, *infamy*. Do what I tell you, Alison. This is your last chance."

He hung up before she could say another word and her heart raced, making her feel nauseous.

Christopher leaned forward, clearly sensing that something more was going on.

"Jared," she said by way of explanation and he leaned back against his seat with a sigh.

"How the hell did he get access to that much cocaine? Let alone slip it into my car?"

She shook her head. "I'm starting to realize that I didn't know him at all."

Christopher snorted. "You have terrible taste in men."

"I can't believe he had you arrested—I'm sorry."

He shrugged. "It's okay. We can just think about it as an adventure."

"Quiet," the officer grunted and they fell silent as he pulled up to the precinct and escorted them inside.

Ali answered their questions as succinctly as possible and said nothing more once Wayde, Christopher's lawyer, arrived and they let her go.

"Excuse me," she said, moving away from the area of cubicles and to the general enquiry desk at the front of the precinct. "I'd like to file a police report—my ex is harassing me."

"I wouldn't do that if I were you," the woman said, blinking her eyes slowly as she looked away and back to her computer screen.

"I'm sorry?"

The officer sighed, pouting her thin lips before shoving a piece of paper through the slot in the plastic screen. "There."

Ali took the paper and looked it over before grabbing one of the pens on the desk to fill it out. When she was done, she handed it back over and the officer nodded vaguely but didn't even bother to look at her as she scrunched the form into a ball and dropped it in the recycling can.

"You can't do that!" Ali gaped at the woman. What the hell was going on?

"Jared's cousin is my husband, you know," she said and Ali just stared.

"So?" Her phone vibrated in her pocket and she wasn't surprised to see her ex's name on the screen. "What?"

"Did I forget to mention that I'm buddies with some of the CYPD? Hell, I'm even related to some of them. Are you starting to get it now, Ali?" He tutted at her and she fought to keep her anger under wraps. "You're a nobody. Your boss may be rich, but money doesn't trump family. Are you ready to be a good little girl?"

Unbelievable. They were all in each other's pocket—corrupt. She shook her head with disgust and had to speak through clenched teeth. "Fine. Make this go away and I'll do what you want."

"Lovely," he said, radiating calm all of a sudden and making goosebumps rise on her skin. "Such a pleasure doing business with you, baby."

She hung up and gave the woman behind the desk a dirty look as she flopped into one of the chairs bolted to the floor and waited for Christopher and Wayde.

"Hey," Christopher said about half-hour later as he caught sight of her sitting there, relief making him slump. "I'm sorry this happened, Ali. We'll figure this out. This isn't over until *he's* the one behind bars."

Chapter Twelve

Tugging at the hem of her dress uncomfortably, Ali stood and made her way to her boss' office after receiving his message asking for her.

She never should have let Jesse talk her into this dress. It was black, tight, and fell to mid-thigh. The only saving grace was that it was a high-turtle-neck style on the top, with full sleeves that at least made it feel a little less exposed. Her skinny-heeled boots had been a bitch to walk to the office in, but she had to admit she did look good. Really good.

There was another man in Christopher's office when she walked in, and the greeting on her boss' mouth cut off in a choked sound as he looked at her.

There was a tense moment of silence where the man at Christopher's side looked between them, a small smirk playing on his full lips.

"You called?" she said, clearing her throat to get rid of the breathy quality to her voice.

"I—yes," Christopher said, his eyes still intent on her as they dropped to her legs and jerked back up again quickly. "This is the friend I was telling you about. Denver, this is Alison."

"A pleasure, I'm sure," the man, Denver, said and Christopher shot him a look that would have made lesser men cower, but Denver's smirk only deepened. It was strange really, he was shockingly handsome and yet Ali couldn't say she felt any particular attraction towards him. Unlike Christopher, who had classic good looks and could have been a James Bond hopeful if the character wasn't such a misogynistic ass, Denver looked like a model. Sharp. Striking. He was all cheekbones and keen eyes.

"Denver runs a software company. They have an app coming out later this year."

She nodded slightly as she approached the desk where Denver was making himself at home. "And you're going to...?"

Denver raised a nearly translucent eyebrow as he shot Christopher a look. "Hack into his accounts remotely, with your help. I might also be able to follow his internet footprint to let us know where he's holed up. Christopher already checked his place out a few days ago after he saw him bothering you and found nobody there—but he could have just missed him I guess."

Brickham her ass. *That* was where he'd gone the day he'd taken off early? Why? To warn Jared away from her after Christopher had seen him grab her? She shot him a look and he shrugged, unrepentant.

"How long will it take?"

"Depends on his security," he muttered, typing away on a brick of a laptop while Christopher seemed to be doing everything he could to avoid looking at her.

She glanced at Denver before moving away from him to approach Christopher by the window that overlooked the city. "I'm sorry. About the dress. My roommates talked me into it, they said I needed to look the part if I was supposed to be seducing you."

He finally turned away from the view to look down at her, wetting his lips as he considered her words. "No, it makes sense."

Did his voice sound a little hoarse?

She opened her mouth but he beat her to it, talking again before she could get another word out.

"Have dinner with me tomorrow."

She raised an eyebrow. "Dinner?"

"It's the third meal of the day."

A low laugh surprised her and she fought the twitching of her lips. "Don't you think it's too soon for me to have won you over?"

Christopher bent lower so his mouth was next to her ear, the tickle of his breath on her skin making her nerves thrum with anticipation. "Nobody who has seen you in that dress today would be surprised that you'd won me over so quickly. So. Dinner tomorrow. Seven?"

Her knees felt a little wobbly as she replayed the low rumble of his voice in her ear before she shook herself and nodded. "Sure. Seven's good."

"Alison," Denver called over to them, "I need some information about Jared."

"Sure," she said, walking back over to him. "Whatever you need."

He peppered her with questions about Jared's hobbies, his pets, his parents, his birthday and interests, and Ali began to realize it was the exact information you might need to answer someone's security questions.

After about an hour or so Denver blew out a long breath. "Fuck."

"What is it?" A muscle ticked in Christopher's jaw and Ali found herself staring at it for longer than was rational.

"He has an authenticator installed. I can duplicate his access key but it's going to take some time."

"We have time," Christopher reassured them both, placing a hand on her shoulder before letting it drop.

"Good, because I'm going to need it."

"So once you get into his cloud, what then?" She bit her lip, not wanting to think about what else Jared might have stored on there.

"Anything that's on his phone or laptop will be on here, unless he's storing it offline, which I doubt—he wouldn't want to lose anything with no backup in his line of work. So once I'm in there, it's a simple matter of wiping it."

A glance at Christopher found his face impassive so she looked back to Denver and said hesitantly, "Ah, you won't have to watch the video will you?"

Denver glanced over her head to look at her boss before focusing back on her. "Of course not."

"Won't he be suspicious if everything suddenly disappears?"

Christopher frowned. "If he's blackmailing you, who knows who else he's doing this to? He might heavily suspect, but it's possible that other people have motive too."

Denver blinked and turned back to his laptop. "Okay, well, you guys just pretend I'm not here and do whatever it is you do. As soon as I'm able to access his cloud I'll let you know." Christopher moved back around the desk and clapped Denver on the back as he watched him type. "Seriously. Stop hovering."

She bit her lip to hide her laugh. God, the last twenty-four hours had been ridiculous. True to his word, Jared had got his buddy on the force to drop the charges. Apparently, they'd reviewed the CCTV of the parking lot and saw the drugs being planted—they'd chalked it up to a prank. A *prank*. At least it was over with for now. Christopher hadn't been formally charged and was released from custody within four hours—that was considered speedy, according to Wayde.

"He's going to know it was me," she murmured and Christopher tilted her chin up to peer into her eyes. More than anything, she didn't want to provoke her ex again. If Denver couldn't solve this for them, she wasn't sure what choice she had left except to leave.

"I won't let him hurt you, or anyone else."

Coming from him, it felt like objective truth somehow.

She nodded and stood, realizing she needed to get back to her desk if she wanted to actually get some work done. "Thank you for this, Denver. I appreciate it, and I owe you one."

He waved off her words. "Please, I've heard so much about you I feel like we're already friends."

Now that surprised her. Christopher had been talking about her to Denver—it had to have been him—but why? What had he said?

She decided it was safer not to know right then. She needed to focus, and around Christopher she became more distracted than ever.

"I'm going to get some work done," she said quickly. "Let me know if you need anything else." She could feel their eyes on her back as she walked out of the room and softly let the office door close behind her.

She could only deal with one thing at a time, and next on her oh-shit list was the fact that she was going for a likely very-public dinner with her boss. He might touch her, all for the ruse, of course, but she wasn't sure how she'd react all the same. As much as she hated to admit it, perhaps for this one she really did need Jesse and Freya's help on what to wear. She should have laid down the ground rules with Christopher back in his office like they'd suggested. *It was likely they wouldn't be necessary anyway*, she told herself. Christopher may be helping her, because they were friends and he was a good man, but it didn't mean he wanted her. Dinner and drinks between friends pretending to be lovers. Easy enough.

Ali caught Christopher's eye as she sat down at her desk and looked up, the heat there making her mouth dry.

Easy, indeed.

Chapter Thirteen

The place Christopher had picked for dinner was built for spectacle, and she felt like she'd already had enough of that tonight. Freya and Jesse had watched her get into the dark town car with Christopher, peeking around the curtains of the window in their living room as if she couldn't see them. At least they meant well. She wasn't sure she could say the same of her colleagues at the office—word had definitely gotten around that she was seeing the boss and the reactions had been mixed. Some people clearly thought it was inappropriate, judging by the dark looks she'd received, others wanted to kiss her ass. Mostly, she wished it would stop.

The Hummingbird was the kind of venue you attended when you wanted to be seen. It was exclusive enough that Ali had never set foot inside, but the atmosphere was surprisingly relaxed—though chic. It was owned by none other than Annabelle DuLoe—Rose's mother, and that had Ali on edge. Christopher was clearly laying the groundwork in case things went wrong and she really did end up attending David and Rose's wedding as his plus-one. *Or,* she considered, *he just likes it here because he's friendly with the owners.*

Despite her concern that they might run into the infamous couple themselves, Ali had to admit that the simple luxury of the bar was stunning.

Christopher placed his hand on the small of her back, guiding her to a booth on the far end of the room opposite the bar in the center. He moved with an ease that spoke of familiarity, and when the bartender nodded in his direction she realized this booth must be his regular. It was lit by what could only be described as mood lighting—dim enough to be flattering but bright enough to read the swirling font on the small menus.

It had been a while since she'd been on a night out. First, her father had passed away and then she'd had the breakup with Jared... she supposed she just hadn't been in the mood for it in a long time.

Her boss looked like a dark god sprawled against the deep purple velvet of the booth, watching her intently like her face was the most fascinating book he'd ever read. She eased out of her jacket and watched him swallow as he took in the steep neckline of the deep blue top Freya and Jesse had bullied her into. It was one of those items of clothing she'd bought because it was pretty and a good color for her, but that she'd never actually been bold enough to wear. It was a strange but nice sensation to watch Christopher run his eyes over her creamy, freckled skin as if he were starving. She pretended not to notice, instead reaching for the menu in front of her and quickly lifting her fingers away from the table when their heat made the glass top fog.

"You're a regular." She didn't phrase it like a question, but he nodded anyway and the faint breeze of the AC made his dark hair sway until a piece dropped onto his forehead to be carelessly brushed away.

"Yes. Plus, I know Annabelle DuLoe so the news that I'm dating again will definitely make its way into the ears of the right people."

"David and Rose you mean."

"I imagine Denver's probably already spilled the beans to Blake. Not," he said hastily, "about our deal. Just that we're seeing each other," he explained and she nodded, willing her racing heart to slow to a more natural rhythm. "News travels fast."

"Did they ask you about the cops?"

Christopher snorted. "Blake thought it was hilarious—I told him it was an unknown prankster."

She tried to smile and it faltered, everything else weighing too heavily on her mind to joke around. "Do you really think Denver can take care of this?" She wasn't sure what made her ask—maybe the fact that he was already taking precautions, thinking two steps ahead, in case it didn't work out like they hoped.

"I think he'll do everything he can," he said simply and the vagueness of the reply would have worried her more if not for his confidence. His face was smooth, unworried, in control. "Do you always worry so much when you go on dates?" He teased and she opened her mouth and closed it. "That was supposed to be rhetorical."

"Sorry. I just don't remember the last time I went on a date."

He squinted. "I think it was about four months ago. You were wearing that red sweater with the little buttons and—" He cut himself off. "That was weird, wasn't it."

"A little." She hadn't realized he'd been paying such close attention. "So are you just really into fashion or something?"

The corners of his lips curled as the bartender approached. "Or something."

They ordered drinks and food and when the bartender left silence fell again. Christopher sighed and slid around the booth so that he was sitting next to her rather than opposite. The heat from his body sank into her skin, and the taste of his cologne got caught on her tongue.

"What?" she asked softly and when he looked at her steadily, she was close enough to count each of his long, dark lashes.

"The point of this dinner," he started, leaning in closer to her, "was to look like you're succeeding at wrapping me around your little finger."

"Right."

"It's hardly convincing when you're sitting across from me with so much tension in your body you might as well be headed to the gallows."

Did she imagine the hitch in his breath when he said the word body? Or was that just wishful thinking?

"So what are you suggesting?" Ali raised one eyebrow

and tried to sound unaffected, but her breath still stuttered when his hand brushed the outside of her thigh beneath the table. It was barely a touch, she would have almost thought she'd imagined it if not for the goosebumps that blazed along her skin and the warmth in the spot he'd touched. One touch shouldn't have her dizzy with want.

"I'm suggesting that you relax," Christopher murmured, leaning in so the words tickled her ear as his hand caressed her thigh again.

"And how do you propose I do that?"

This was a dangerous game. If they weren't careful, they were going to get in way over their heads. The fact that he was her boss suddenly felt like a flimsy excuse, easily brushed aside as his fingers closed around her knee before coasting higher.

What wasn't flimsy, however, was the very real threat they faced if Jared didn't buy that they were together and going along with his demands.

Her eyes fluttered as Christopher's hand neared the hem of her skirt before she caught it with her own, reason raising its ugly head.

"You don't need to do this. I can get a drink, I'll relax, we can sell this without—" His hand slipped underneath her skirt and she forgot how to breathe as desire flooded every one of her senses. "Christopher," she gasped, and knew she should mean it as an admonishment to put an end to this madness, but she didn't want it to end. For once, she wanted to revel in it.

"Nobody forces me to do anything I don't want to do." His words in her ear were so close to a growl she shivered.

"So let me give you this, Alison. You need it as much as I do."

She whimpered, a tiny sound yet he didn't miss it.

"Ali," his whisper was heated and her imagination ran away from her as she wondered if this was what he sounded like in bed.

"Yes."

Warmth spread over her as he dragged his thumb over the sensitive spot on her inner thigh, sending a flood of wetness between her legs. Normally she would never do this. Not in public. But the booth was dark and secluded, and with Christopher she felt safe.

His index finger skimmed the outside of her underwear and she jumped, not with surprise but desire and he chuckled.

"I don't see what's funny," she said breathlessly as he began to trace languid circles over the top of the fabric separating them.

"I was worried you wouldn't want this as much as I did," he said and then gave a low groan that had her clenching around nothing as he pressed his fingers against her more thoroughly.

"And you're not worried about that anymore?" At this point, she wasn't even sure what she was saying, just that she wanted to hear his voice again. The deep silk of it did something to her.

"No."

"No?"

"It's hard to be worried about anything when you're

dripping so much for me. My fingers are wet without even having gone inside your underwear. Yet."

He retrieved his hand and leaned back to watch her as he slid two fingers into his mouth and sucked.

"If I thought we could get away with it I would bury my face in that sweet pussy right now." A smirk curled around his lips as he leaned in close, eyes running over her face. "Oh, you like the sound of that, don't you Ali? Another time," he promised and the thought of this happening more than once nearly made her pass out.

She made no reply but the small smile he gave her said he knew the answer regardless. Sliding lower in his seat, Christopher grabbed her right ankle and crooked her leg to one side, hooking it over his own before dragging his hand upwards. Her skin felt like it was vibrating in anticipation as he rocked one finger over the center of her. Her underwear was so soaked she could feel it sticking to her. She needed relief. Now.

Deft fingers pushed her panties to one side and the cool air hitting her in public felt erotic in a way she'd never experienced before.

"I wish I could see you right now," he said, voice hoarse as one finger slowly moved to touch her, sliding over her sensitive bud before he dipped it shallowly inside of her. "So wet, Ali."

She tried to keep her breathing even and failed spectacularly as two fingers pressed more firmly against her clit, squeezing and pinching it softly between them and sending pulsing waves of pleasure through her.

"Do you think you can keep quiet for me, Ali?"

Christopher asked as the wet sounds of her pussy drifted up towards them. His fingers moved quicker, coaxing her hips into a rocking motion she couldn't hold back.

"Y-Yes," she whispered and he tutted.

"Then I'm not doing a good enough job."

The angle of his hand shifted so his thumb pressed down on her clit as two fingers slid easily inside her.

"So hot, so wet for me," his words were uttered so low that she knew he hadn't meant to say them aloud. "Does that feel good, Ali? Do you like it when my fingers fuck you like this?"

Oh god, never had she dreamed that she would be here with her boss, letting him speak to her like this. Maybe she'd fantasized about it one or two times, but she'd never thought it would actually happen.

He crooked his fingers and a low moan stole its way out of her throat, choking off abruptly when the server appeared from nowhere with their drinks.

Christopher smiled like he didn't have his fingers in her pussy and she tried to look relaxed, though she could only imagine what she looked like right now. Face flushed, hair probably starting to frizz a little from where her head had been tilted back and rubbing against the velvet of the booth...

A wicked look gleamed in Christopher's eye and he maneuvered a third finger into her, pushing in and out of her faster as their drinks were set down with a soft thump and she tried to keep her mouth shut.

As soon as the server left, he praised her. "You did so

good. Kept nice and quiet while I fucked your pussy in front of him."

"Christopher," she begged and he licked his lips and nodded.

His fingers curled, rubbing against the sensitive inner wall as he increased the pressure on her clit until she was seeing stars. He stopped before she could fall over the edge completely and instead began a steady pace as his fingers worked her.

Her muscles tensed and the heat inside her coiled, ready to snap. He increased his speed and she clenched around him, her orgasm sweeping over her so quickly she was breathless, unable to make a sound as her body shook.

"There," he said with more than a hint of smugness in his voice, "aren't you more relaxed now?" He reached for a napkin and used it to wipe away some of the wetness that coated her inner thighs.

The truth was that yes, she did feel more relaxed. The problem? She couldn't imagine never doing that again.

Chapter Fourteen

B y the time they finished dinner, the paparazzi were waiting for them. Christopher had been right, their presence at *The Hummingbird* hadn't gone unnoticed and the flash of bright lights immediately overwhelmed her as they stepped out of the alcove and into a press of bodies eager to get close.

A warm arm wrapped around her shoulders as Christopher pulled her into him and tucked her head to his chest so he could better shield her.

"Get back," he demanded and the power in his voice was lethal. Despite the orgasm she'd just had, she found herself getting worked up again. "Move, now."

The crowd parted and they stepped into an idling town car. Christopher's was still in the impound, apparently it took longer to release objects than people, so they were stuck using a car service for the time being.

The trip to her place was unfortunately short and she half-wished he would take her home with him—but that wasn't in the cards. The orgasm may have been real, and so was the attraction between them, but the relationship was fake and she couldn't let herself forget it.

As soon as she got home, Ali was ready for a long shower and bed.

Jesse looked up at her as the door closed, her greeting faltering as she caught a look at her. "Jeez. Did he take you rock climbing on your first date or something?"

"What? No. Why?" She threw her keys onto the kitchen counter as she kicked off her heels.

"Well then why are you all red and sweaty—" Jesse's eyes widened as a cat-like grin flashed across her face. "Freya! Come quick! And bring the bottle!"

"Jesse—" Ali protested but by then her other roommate had opened her door and joined them.

"Oh my god, I thought you were joking," Freya said as she grinned at them both and grabbed the bottle of champagne she'd had in the fridge for months.

"I thought you were saving that for a special occasion," she said, confused, and Freya and Jesse wore identical looks of glee.

"Yep! The occasion being: Ali slept with her boss!"

"Are you serious?"

They nodded their heads and Freya gave her a kiss on the cheek as she grabbed three glasses from the cupboard above the cereal.

"Ali, you're a horrible liar. We knew you were in denial, so we bought the bottle and ran a bet."

At first she was outraged, her mouth dropping open as

she took a breath to scold them, but then curiosity got the best of her. "Who won?"

"By the looks of things, I'd say you babe." Jesse waggled her eyebrows and Ali snorted.

"You lasted longer than either of us predicted."

"Gee, thanks," Ali muttered before accepting the glass of bubbles being thrust toward her.

"We need details."

"Was he a good kisser?"

"How many times did you do it?"

"I've heard his cock is massive so we obviously need verification from you."

Alison shot Jesse a look for that final comment and then sighed. "We didn't have sex."

They both paused, their glasses halfway to their mouths and an accusatory look in their eyes.

"Spill."

"He, um, touched me. Under the table."

Jesse blew out a whistle. "Damn, girl. You had me worried for a second that we opened the bottle too soon."

"It counts?"

"Sex doesn't have to be just penetrative," Freya said matter of factly and Ali nodded.

"I think you were right," Ali said with a sigh. "We should have established boundaries. I'm going to go shower and turn in for the night. Enjoy the champagne," she said, downing her drink and nodding to the glasses they held as her roommates clinked them together.

After her shower, Ali settled in her room and decided to let her hair air dry naturally. It meant it would be curlier than usual tomorrow but she couldn't bring herself to care, her mind was busy elsewhere.

The blue candle on her bedside sat to her right and she inhaled as she lit it, enjoying the scent of ocean and cotton as she propped herself up against the headboard and reached for her top drawer.

Truthfully, it had been a much better night than she had been anticipating when she'd left the apartment. She'd been expecting to feel out of place, awkward, and tense— and she had, a little, but the truth was that around Christopher she always felt at ease. He had an air of calm about him that she had found soothing from the very moment she'd met him, like he was the eye at the center of the storm, calm amidst the chaos.

But right then, the last thing Ali felt was calm. All she could think about was Christopher's hands on her body, his fingers between her thighs, the roughness of his voice when he'd whispered filthy things in her ear. She wanted more. But she couldn't have it—not if they wanted to keep things uncomplicated between them, both for the sake of the ruse and their professional lives.

So Ali grabbed the two-pronged toy and let it massage her clit as it vibrated before easing it inside herself.

Christopher had been good with his hands, attentive, drinking up every one of her reactions and repeating whatever had pleased her the most. It made her wonder just how attentive he might be elsewhere in the bedroom.

She panted slightly as she ground her hips against the toy, imagining it was her boss' mouth, his tongue, tasting her.

Jesse had obviously got Ali wondering about other areas Christopher might be generous in too. After he'd made her come, they'd eaten dinner and he'd stayed by her side instead of moving back to the other seat. The bulge in his dark jeans had been noticeable, but he hadn't seemed to care if she returned the favor, like he was sated enough from having made her fall apart for him.

Ali tilted her hand and let her body take over as she thought about the way the material of her boss' shirt had stretched across his chest, loosely buttoned to reveal a tease of bare skin, the way he'd sucked on his fingers to taste her and the longing in his face when he told her how much he wanted to devour her.

Her body shuddered and her face felt warm as she slumped back, easing the toy out of her with a satisfied sigh. It had taken the edge off, but she got the feeling she would need to stock up on batteries if she was going to keep her head in the game and her hands to herself.

Chapter Fifteen

I t wasn't often that she stopped for coffee on the way to work, but she needed the extra fortification in order to face her boss after the things he'd done to her last night. Naturally though, she only got a few paces inside the door and within sight of the counter of *Lola's* before a tentative voice sounded from behind her.

"Alison?"

She turned and felt her mouth drop open. "You don't come here." Her cheeks heated immediately and she scrambled to apologize. "I'm sorry, I meant that I haven't seen you in here before and this place is kind of a favorite of mine."

Rose DuLoe laughed and it was a sultry sound that had a few heads turning as she brushed her blonde sheet of hair back from her face. "I'm not local, no. It's part of my therapy, trying new things and going to new places. I've still got Noah with me though."

Ali smiled, tilting her head slightly. If it wasn't for the

fact that her ex-boyfriend wanted her to screw up this woman's wedding, she might have enjoyed the conversation more. It was refreshing to hear someone so openly discussing their mental health, though Rose had become somewhat known for it in the year after being targeted by a stalker. "Let me get you a coffee," she said as the barista called her forwards and Rose blinked and then smiled.

"Thank you."

They placed their order and took a seat at a nearby table to wait for them to be ready. It felt beyond strange to be sitting in a coffee shop with Rose, like being out with a celebrity.

"Forgive me for prying," she said and Ali raised an eyebrow. "But I heard you were at *The Hummingbird* yesterday with Chris."

Ali nodded. "Yeah, it's lovely in there."

Rose smiled slightly. "I'm glad he's dating again. I told Blake we should set him up with someone but he said Chris was already into some redhead at work." A glint in her eye made Ali sit up straight as the words swam around her head. *Some redhead.* Fuck. Christopher *liked* her? Or was there another redhead her boss often noticed?

She wracked her brains and couldn't think of anyone else, and it filled her with a smug sort of satisfaction.

"So I'm glad you're finally giving him a shot," Rose finished and Ali nearly did a double-take.

"I had no idea he even liked me," she said and then amended hastily, "Until recently, obviously."

Rose snorted. "I'm pleased for you both all the same."

They stood for their coffees and Ali smiled. "Well, I've got to get into the office. It was nice seeing you."

"You too," Rose said, light brown eyes assessing her keenly. "I look forward to getting to know you better. Thanks for the coffee."

Why did that sound more like a threat than anything else?

THE COFFEE WAS SITTING ODDLY in her stomach as she found her way to her desk. Not only was almost every eye in the office watching her, but she was worried about how she was supposed to act around Christopher after last night, especially with the info Rose had just dropped on her.

That nervousness immediately faded once she saw Denver in her boss' office talking to him and she hurried over to them, knocking quickly on the door before pushing it open and then freezing when they both turned to look at her.

"Um, good morning. I was just wondering if it worked?" Her hands twisted into fists at her side and she did her best to try and get them to uncurl.

Denver smiled, his teeth perfectly white and even, highlighting his cupid's bow. "Finished deleting everything this morning."

It felt like she had been walking around with weights attached to her legs that had been suddenly cut, leaving her feeling ten pounds lighter. She sat down in the chair opposite Christopher's desk before she could fall down and sucked in a few breaths before springing up again to hug Denver hard.

"Thank you."

He had stiffened at her leap but relaxed when she squeezed him and pulled away.

"You're not out of the woods yet, but I'm glad I could help. I can't guarantee that he doesn't have other copies stashed away somewhere though."

Her boss' jaw was strangely tight as he watched Denver put some space between them and she winced, realizing she had probably overstepped charging in here the way she had.

"Sorry, I'll let you get back to your meeting."

"Wait," Christopher said, dark brows slanting down into a frown as he stepped toward her. "Don't you want to discuss your next steps?"

"Isn't it over?" Biting her lip, she slowly sank back down into the chair when Christopher gestured to it.

"We need to be sure this is finished before we make any other moves."

"You want me to meet him again." Did her heart always race this much? She fanned her face but nodded. "Okay. I'll message him now."

Typically, her phone was buried right at the bottom of her purse, and by the time she pulled it free her hands were shaking with nerves. She wanted so badly for this to be done with and over, but Christopher was right. They had to make sure Jared wasn't going to try something else.

His reply came back to her almost immediately and

she had to imagine he was seething that his files were gone, if he even knew yet.

Alison: We need to talk

Jared: I already told you that the time for talking is over. Don't make me remind you, Alison.

"He doesn't think we need to meet again," she told the two men lurking at her side, trying to keep her voice steady even as panic started to rear its head.

"Just tell him you have information for him," Denver suggested, taking in the shaking of her hands with concern.

"Okay," she whispered before repeating herself louder. "Okay."

Alison: I have an update for you. Information.

Jared: Send it now.

Alison: Can't. Need to meet.

There was a pause as he clearly mulled over her words before his reply came again and she let out a breath of relief.

Jared: Fine. Arthur's. 3 PM.

She held up the phone so that Christopher and Denver could read the message and then sagged against the chair. Logically, she knew there was no reason for her to be shaking this much. She had dated this guy for nearly three months and had never worried for her safety. But it felt different now, like the gloves were off and masks dropped. She wasn't sure what Jared was capable of anymore.

Voices were talking quietly around her but she

couldn't focus on them, all she could hear was her own labored breathing. Was this a panic attack? She'd had one when she'd found out her dad had died too, but otherwise she wasn't usually prone to anxiety or panic attacks. Though, these were extenuating circumstances and admittedly she'd been feeling on edge a lot recently.

"Ali." It was a quiet murmur from a deep voice, its timbre sinking into her bones and momentarily quelling the shaking until it started up again. Warm hands slid under her chin and deep brown eyes took up the whole of her vision. They had surprising streaks of amber that would have been impossible to view until she was as close to his face as this, but she knew these eyes familiarly, fondly, anyway.

"Christopher," she whispered and he shushed her as her head continued to spin.

"Just breathe for me, Alison."

What was he talking about? Were those not her gasping breaths she could hear?

"Alison, breathe."

Her eyes flitted around the room but saw nothing, it was a hazy blur as her vision darkened inexplicably.

"Breathe!"

The sharpness of the command forced her to suck in a deep, measured breath and the darkness in the corners of her eyes faded as oxygen began to filter through her system again.

Christopher was on his knees in front of her, peering into her eyes as he ran one hand absently over her hair, her cheek, as if searching for injuries that weren't there.

"I won't let him hurt you," he said quietly and she nodded, her body still feeling out of sync with the rest of her mind. "Denver and I will be there the whole time, okay? You won't be alone."

She bit her lip to stop its trembling and stiffened as her boss tugged her roughly to his chest before she relaxed, her head resting on his shoulder.

Denver stood near the windows, like he'd backed off to give them privacy, and a soft smile was on his face as he watched them.

She pulled away and smoothed a hand over her hair before nodding to herself. "I'm okay. I can do this."

"We've got a few hours until you need to meet him later, so why don't you head home and—"

"No," she interrupted, and then smiled slightly. "I need to stay busy. But thank you. I appreciate it."

Christopher nodded and a silence descended that felt awkward. Probably because she'd essentially just had a breakdown in her boss' office.

"Okay then," she said, awkwardly standing and smoothing the sleek hem of her dress. "You know where I'll be."

They watched her leave and she didn't turn around, knowing what she'd find on their faces—a mixture of pity and concern. She understood it, but that didn't mean she had to like it.

"Everything's going to be fine," she muttered as she sat at her desk, and didn't let herself examine why that felt so much like a lie.

Chapter Sixteen

"Arms up," Denver said and she obeyed as he looped a wire around her stomach and taped it in place just under the front of her bra between her breasts.

Wearing a wire to this meeting seemed a little overkill to her, but if it gave her any evidence she could actually use against Jared so she could take this to the police then it would be worth it. Though who she'd even approach that wasn't in his pocket, she wasn't sure. She had no idea where Denver had gotten the equipment from, and when she'd asked he'd just shrugged and said he knew people.

Christopher was standing off to one side and she'd felt his eyes on her more than once, but when she'd looked to him he'd seemed preoccupied with making sure Denver wasn't getting handsy. It was almost like he was... jealous.

"We'll be right out here," Denver said as she tugged her top back into place and twisted her hands together nervously. "If you need us, just text okay?"

She nodded and blew out a long breath as Christopher approached, his dark eyes taking her measure. She tilted her chin and gave him a firmer nod. She could do this. They were *so close* to being done with all of this.

"You've got this," he said quietly and the words were still ringing through her head as she walked into one of the best burger joints in the city.

Arthur's was never really ever quiet, which was great if you didn't want to be overheard. Unfortunately, it rendered the recording device Denver had insisted she bring with her in case Jared said anything incriminating absolutely pointless.

They'd arrived at the meet nearly twenty minutes early after Christopher had seen her stress cleaning her desk for the fifth time and declared they should get ahead of any traffic.

It had seemed stupid not to walk, but she hadn't argued. The sooner this meeting was over with, the better.

Ali looked up from checking her phone just as a tall frame slid into the seat of the cheap plastic booth opposite her.

Jared.

"What have you got for me?"

She slid an envelope over the table and watched as he lifted it curiously before slipping it open to find a blank sheet of paper.

"Explain."

His voice had gone cold, colder than usual anyway and she bit the inside of her cheek until she tasted blood before replying.

"It's yours."

"It's blank," he gritted out and she wondered how she had ever found this man attractive.

"Yes. So is your cloud. You don't have anything on me, and I only came here to tell you in person that our business is done. Don't contact me again or I'll call the police."

She was already half-out of her seat when she stiffened at the sound of his laughter. Dread made it hard to swallow as she looked back at him and the humor faded from his face as he leaned across the sticky vinyl table.

"Sit back down."

She did as he asked and tried not to flinch when he continued to crowd her space.

"I mean, it was a good try, Ali. But you forgot the most crucial thing when it comes to a war like this—*know thy enemy.*"

Under other circumstances she might have laughed at his corniness, but he was being utterly serious. And he was right, she didn't know him. That much was becoming abundantly clear.

"I did my research. You think I don't know who your boss' bestie is? I took precautions, baby."

She flinched at the familiar nickname, hating the memories it conjured and the fact that he'd been able to hurt her with it even after everything.

"You're bluffing," she snapped but the glint of triumph in his eyes left her feeling unsure.

He pulled his phone out of his coat pocket and tapped

at the screen for a second before turning it to show her. That was it. The full video.

She knew she was blushing, could feel the hot sting of tears in her eyes as she watched herself on screen, watching him use her as he shot a grin at the camera over her head.

He wasn't bluffing.

"I take it we understand each other?" She nodded and he smiled, eyes alight with a brightness that was almost feverish. Was he on something? "Excellent. Now, Ali. I don't want to hear from you again unless I contact you first. This has been fun and you've amused me, so I won't hurt your mother this time."

The casual way that he spoke about it made acid churn in her stomach. "Leave her out of it."

"That depends entirely on you." He smiled like this was any other pleasant conversation and then stood, licking his lips. "Seeing as I'm here, it would be rude not to get fries, right?"

Jared walked away, his lanky form easily blending into the crowd surrounding the register and for a second she just sat there, her eyes swimming and saliva filling her mouth before she scrambled up and pushed towards the exit.

Christopher and Denver found her in the lot ten minutes later, crouched behind the building and throwing up the bile in her stomach.

The thought that she had let that piece of crap put his hands on her, that he'd been inside of her, smirking up at the camera... She knew he'd betrayed her, obviously, but to see it tossed out there like that made her feel the rush of rage and pain all over again.

Ten scalding hot showers wouldn't have been enough to make her feel clean.

"It's not over, is it." Christopher looked grim, the corner of his mouth tugging down as he ran a hand through his hair.

"No," she managed, "it's not."

"And we just poked the bear."

Christopher shot Denver an irritated look, his jaw clenching and unclenching as he paced in front of them. "Did he say what he wants you to do now?"

The world felt less wavy now that she'd puked up her guts, but she still knew she couldn't go back to work in this state. "No. He just said he would contact me."

"So for now, we wait."

She took a step and staggered slightly and Denver caught her with one warm arm around her waist. He let go quickly and she blinked at how fast he moved. "Is it okay with you if I head home? I promise I'll catch up on my work later."

Christopher, who had been looking at Denver somewhat intently, immediately softened. "Of course. Look, Ali, you're only in this position because of your connection to me. So I'm sorry, and I promise I will do everything I can to fix it. Go home. Rest. Take the rest of the week if you like."

She smiled weakly. "It's not your fault either. It's his."

Christopher shrugged and said nothing else as they walked back to the town car. "We'll drop you home."

She nodded her thanks and then relaxed against the leather seats, exhausted. She didn't even realize she'd fallen asleep until a horn sounded when someone drove past. They were parked outside of her apartment and Christopher was looking outside, unaware she was awake.

She didn't move, just content to watch him, when Denver spoke softly.

"Are you sure about all of this? You could try and talk to him again. Blake is going to be pissed if you leak anything to the press, man."

Her boss lifted one shoulder and let it fall. "Last time I tried to talk to him I got arrested. Blake can be pissed all he wants. She's worth it."

She's worth it. God, she couldn't explain how badly she'd needed to hear that, to know that someone thought that outside of maybe her mom.

They fell silent again and she decided it would be safe to 'wake up'. As soon as she stirred, Christopher's eyes flew to hers.

"Hey, we're here."

"You should have woken me," she said after checking the time on her phone.

"You needed to sleep."

They watched each other silently in the near-dark as the sun slunk lower in the sky and it wasn't until Denver cleared his throat that she startled back into action.

"Well, I should get inside."

"Yeah," he said, but there was something burning hot

in his eyes that made her hesitate before she pushed open the door and walked to her apartment building.

Things hadn't gone to plan from the very beginning. She could only hope that they weren't going to get hurt too badly in whatever came next.

Chapter Seventeen

"Didn't Christopher tell you to stay here and rest?" Jesse asked the next morning as Ali poured coffee into her to-go cup.

She shrugged. "He said I could, not that I *had* to."

"And you don't think you need to take a beat?" Freya asked gently from her place at the table as she picked at a fruit salad.

"I took a beat last night." It was true, she'd come in and updated her roommates on what had happened and then essentially crashed. "I need to be there today."

"Are you sure—"

"I'm sure." Her smile was tight. She knew they meant well, but she knew what she needed right now better than them. She was the one trapped in her own head. Initially, she'd had every intention of following Christopher's advice, but the longer she'd stayed in bed the more her mind had refused to quiet. She needed to be busy, or she'd lose her shit. It was no good for her to sit around at home stressed and worrying. "Have a good day," she told them before striding out of the door and down the stairs to the apartment complex entrance.

It was pleasant outside and the light blouse and pants she'd chosen to wear were perfect for the faint breeze and surprising sunshine. Sometimes it was the little things.

She'd only been at the office for about an hour when Christopher walked past and did a double-take.

"Ali, you're here?"

"Should I not be?"

"No—I mean, you can do whatever you'd like. I was just surprised is all."

She nodded but didn't stay anything else and he swept a stray piece of hair out of his eyes before continuing past her desk and into his office.

She spent the next hour and a half going through the build up of emails in her inbox, and then rearranging Christopher's schedule for a few last-minute meetings he was going to need to take. Once everything was in order, she stood and knocked on his open office door, ready to do what she should have done at the start of the week.

"Ali," Christopher greeted from behind his desk as he glanced up from the computer screen. "Everything okay?"

"Everything's fine," she said and was impressed by how convincing she sounded. "I'd like to tender my resignation, effective immediately. I've set up meetings for you with the three prospective candidates I picked out before, I think you'll be pleased with the choices."

His eyes had flown wide as she spoke, leaving his usual

calm demeanor looking ruffled. Touchable. "You said you'd give me time."

"And I did."

"You gave me less than a week," he said, throwing his hands up in the air and she tried not to be fascinated at his lack of cool—it was probably one of the only times she'd seen him lose it.

"Sure, and now we don't have any plans left to work with. We tried deleting the video, we tried talking to David—Jared is smart. There's no need for you to be wrapped up in this. In fact, I'm the one complicating things! If he was just targeting you it would be easy to amp up security or take him down, but he's got that recording and he knows me, how I think and—"

"Breathe," he said, cutting her off and she sucked down the air greedily, realizing she'd been spiraling.

"Look, I'm grateful for your help, but now that we don't have anything else we can try I think it's best that I leave and just let the chips fall where they may."

"No," he said simply, reclining back in his leather chair and watching her steadily.

"*No?*" She laughed but it was mostly out of shock rather than humor.

"You're giving up." He stood and walked around the desk toward her and she inhaled sharply at how close they were standing."You're letting him win."

"No," she growled. "I'm taking the choice away from him and making it *mine*."

"By running away?"

"I'm not—"

"I asked you for time," he said—pleaded, really. "Why can't you give me it?"

"Why does it matter so much to you that I stay?" she countered and he looked away, the muscle in his jaw ticking as he remained silent for a beat longer than usual.

"Because I need you," he said eventually and her breathing sounded loud in her own ears.

"What does that mean?"

"It means I'm not ready to let you go, damn it. It's hard to play the long game when you're not here, Ali."

The long game? "I'm just some game to you?"

"You know that's not what I meant."

She did. But it wasn't helpful to hear that right then, when she was trying to leave. When she was trying to protect him.

He took a step forward and she moved a step back. A hint of a smile tugged up one side of his mouth as he nodded slowly, like he finally understood some missing piece of information. She really wished he'd enlighten her. "I see."

"See what?" she huffed out and watched in confusion as he walked away from her, back to his desk. Had he decided she wasn't worth the trouble after all?

He picked up the corded phone on his desk and she was surprised how much it hurt, being dismissed like the conversation was just over.

She turned toward the door just as he spoke.

"Hey, Blake? I need a favor and Rose is really not going to like it." He laughed and Ali turned around slowly, eyes narrowed in suspicion at the faux-innocent look on her boss' face.

"Yeah, nothing major. I just do want a plus one after all." He nodded at whatever his friend was saying before smiling. "Excellent. I owe you one." He laughed good-naturedly before thanking him again and hanging up. "Problem solved."

"The problem is *not* solved! I don't want to give Jared what he wants. I'm not doing this!"

"You don't have to give Jared anything," Christopher said calmly and his cool exterior made her want to shake him, or rumple his hair, rough him up a little so he looked as much of a mess as she felt. "Same deal as before," he continued, "you give me time to handle this. In the meantime we feed Jared small info. Innocuous stuff to keep him at bay but not enough to really piss off Rose."

Ali winced. Rose DuLoe was not someone she wanted to make an enemy of.

"Christopher—"

"You want to protect me, the company, I get that. I love that. But not at your expense, Ali. I promise you that Jared is going to pay—so, for now, let me protect you." By the time he finished speaking he was back in front of her, his breath whispering across her lips and his warmth invading her senses until she had to close her eyes before she sank into temptation.

"Okay." If they hadn't been standing so close, she never would have felt his sigh of relief. But she did, and she wasn't sure what to do with it.

Her eyes opened again slowly and she instantly

wanted to close them again because the sight of Christopher, of her boss, standing there and looking like he'd burn the world to the ground if it meant protecting her was almost enough to crumble any strength or sense of self-preservation she had left.

She took a step back and the mask of calm fell over his face once more. Good. It was for the best.

She'd been far too free with her heart in the past. This time, she wasn't going to be as foolish.

Chapter Eighteen

"You don't need to worry about me, sweetheart. I've got Caleb keeping me company."

"I'm glad," Ali said, rolling her eyes as she folded some laundry on her bed and shifted the phone to her other shoulder, tilting her head to keep it in place. "Just promise me you're not going anywhere without him."

Her mom gave what could only be described as a girlish giggle. "Trust me, we're joined at the hip," she said slyly and Ali laughed.

"Safety first."

"Exactly. How're things with you though, kiddo? How's work?"

Work, of course, made her think about Christopher. It had been... Well, to look at Christopher you would think the last week and a half had gone perfectly after he'd cajoled her into staying at *Horizons* for a while longer. The truth was that it was awkward. He'd looked at her a little too closely and seen more than she wanted.

There was no undoing it. Her only consolation was that she'd got close enough to see the version of himself he normally kept locked down under a facade of confidence and calm.

The main problem? She'd liked what she'd seen, even if she shouldn't want it. Even if whatever she was feeling for him would only end in heartbreak because this was supposed to be *pretend*, damn it.

"Sweetie?"

She cleared her throat, realizing she'd been thinking too hard for too long. "Work is fine."

"Has anything more happened with that bastard?"

Ali knew exactly who her mom was referring to, it was the same thing she always called Jared now whenever they spoke. Though truthfully, her mom had never been a fan of him. "It's being handled." She hoped.

"Okay. Well, keep me updated. You know I worry."

"I know. Love you," she added and felt a little better when they hung up.

THE INVITATION ARRIVED the same day that her first message from Jared did. She hadn't heard from him since they'd met at *Arthur's* a week and a half ago. He kept it brief and to the point.

Jared: Outfits, guests, I want pictures. She has a white folder filled with wedding details, find it and take photos.

Attached to his message was a photo clearly taken

through her mom's front window, but after an initial flood of panic she stilled and peered closer, zooming in.

"Huh," she said aloud, tilting her head. Sneaky bastard. Jared wasn't anywhere near her mom's place—Ali would bet her life on it. Because in the corner of the photo, just in frame, was the vase her mom had broken last week while she was on the phone with her—leading to an hour-long rant about getting older and her ass getting bigger. It wasn't the kind of lecture she could forget fast. So he must have taken this photo a while ago, probably while they were still together. *The betrayals just keep piling up,* she mused morosely.

She locked her phone with a sigh and felt her head rest against the cool wood of the desk for a moment before the soft sound of a throat clearing made her sit up.

"I'm guessing you've heard the news then."

She shot her boss a look as he leaned against her desk, looking far more attractive than he had any right to be. "It's Rose DuLoe and David Blake's engagement party, I think it's probably already hit the radio stations."

"Has he messaged you?" Christopher asked, deciding to ignore her sarcasm.

"Yes," she said a little more quietly. "He wants me to go and take photos. He said something about a book of wedding plans?"

Christopher nodded. "Yeah she's been carrying that thing around with her constantly. I'm surprised you haven't seen it."

"I don't keep up with that kind of stuff," she said with a shrug and her boss' lips twitched.

"It's on Friday," he said eventually and she nodded, suppressing a groan. "What, too busy to go to the most sought-after engagement party of the year? Hell, probably the last five years?"

Ali rolled her eyes as she stood and collected her purse. "It sounds delightful."

"Where are you going?" There was a tightness to his voice that made her pause as she walked past him, analyzing his face to try and find the source of it. Was it anger? No, she decided, the pinched look in his eyes looked more like concern than irritation.

"Well, apparently I'm going to need a dress for an event on Friday and I don't think I've taken a lunch break away from my desk maybe ever? So, I'm going shopping."

"Shopping?" he said doubtfully, tilting his eyebrows up until they nearly reached his hairline.

"Mm," she said as she popped a hip cockily. "It's this thing you do where you give a store money and in return they let you take stuff."

"Well, do you need a second opinion?"

Now *that* threw her. "You want to come shopping."

"Sure," he said easily and her mind flashed back to all the times she'd had to *beg* Jared to come to the mall with her.

"With me," she repeated and he nodded like she was the one who was slow on the uptake.

Clearly worried her shock was disdain, he stepped forward and raised an eyebrow. "I'll even pay for the dress."

She pretended to think about it, biting her lip and

sagging her shoulders for dramatic effect. "Fine, but only if you'll drive us too."

"Deal," he said smugly, adjusting his tie and tugging on the ends of his suit sleeves. He'd gotten his car back from the cops at the end of the previous week and she knew he'd been thrilled to drive himself places again instead of using the car service.

She followed him down the corridor and jumped when he caught her hand in his as they strolled past her colleagues, prompting more looks of envy, disapproval, and surprise.

They could definitely have taken a shorter route, but Christopher seemed content to parade her around like a prize.

"Enjoy yourself?" she asked when they stepped into the elevator that would take them down to the parking garage.

"Immensely," he said with a smirk and she had to look away before she blushed.

"I was only kidding you know," she said when the doors opened and they stepped out. "Not about you coming with me," she amended when he looked a little disappointed. "About buying me a dress. I have my own money."

His eyes crinkled at the corners when he laughed. "Nope, I insist. What's the point of having money if I can't use it to buy beautiful dresses for even more beautiful women?"

She raised an eyebrow but couldn't hide her

amusement as he opened the passenger side of the car and shut it once she'd safely climbed in.

THEY'D BEEN WALKING around the out-of-town mall for over two hours and Ali was kind of ready to kill her boss. She'd liked the first dress she'd tried on, but Christopher had insisted it wasn't 'the one'—whatever that meant. And so the procession of dresses began.

"Some say that you can still find the spirit of the boss and his assistant walking the halls of the mall, searching for the perfect dress to this day," Ali said in her most ghostly voice as Christopher approached the table she'd claimed in the food court with their frozen yogurt.

"You can have any dress you want," he said as he licked a long line of frozen yogurt off of the plastic spoon and she watched the motion of his tongue a little too closely. "I'm just waiting for you to say something more enthusiastic than *this is okay* or *this is fifty percent off*," he mimicked in a high falsetto that sounded nothing like her voice. "Money isn't an issue. Hell, pick the most expensive dress in the store, if you like. I just want you to wear something you genuinely like and feel good in."

She swallowed a too-big bite of fro-yo and cringed when it made her teeth ache. She hadn't really expected him to buy her a dress, or shoes, or any other number of things Christopher had pointed out to her as they walked around. Sure, he had the money for it, she'd just never realized she would have trouble accepting it. She'd always been self-sufficient, she supposed old habits were hard to break.

"Come on," he said, standing and leading her to one of the only formal dress shops they hadn't been into yet. "If you don't find something you like in this one then I'm going to have something custom designed for you and rush delivered and it will be *hideously* expensive." He smirked at her look of horror and led the way into the store before seating himself on one of the tiny chairs in front of a row of curtained dressing rooms.

She took her time, wandering through the racks and inspecting the dresses until a smiley sales associate came over and asked if she needed help. The truth was that she did—it wasn't often she had to wear black tie to anything. Business casual or smart-business office wear was pretty much her go-to for the majority of events she had to attend. Black-tie parties and custom designer dresses were a whole other world that just didn't come naturally to her.

Eventually she made her way to the dressing rooms, and the assistant helped her clamber in and out of three dresses before she tried on the fourth and stopped to stare.

Damn him for being right, but it suddenly felt like this dress was *the one.*

The sales associate grinned. "You look gorgeous and I'm not just saying that for commission."

She laughed slightly breathlessly as she twisted in front of the mirror, assessing it from all angles. But, simply put, it was stunning. *She* was stunning in it.

The dress was a deep emerald, strapless, and with a

ruffle around the waist that emphasized her curves while the silky material made her look sleek and polished.

"Are you ready to show your boyfriend?" The woman asked, her smile made all the perkier by the gap in her bottom teeth.

"Oh, he's not my—" She caught herself and just nodded. "Yeah, I'm ready."

Chapter Nineteen

S he slid open the soft beige curtain and stepped out. It was a good thing Christopher had finished his frozen yogurt already, because he accidentally dropped the empty cup straight onto the floor when he saw her.

She twirled slowly so he could get the full effect. "What do you think?"

He swallowed and said nothing and she began to worry that she'd made a mistake— maybe she had terrible taste—when he suddenly stood and then halted like he couldn't move any closer.

"You are..." He swallowed again like the words were stuck in his throat. "Everything," he finished, breathless, and her pulse quickened at the way he drank her in.

The air between them seemed to fill with electricity, like a tangible pull that was urging her towards him even as she tried to deny it.

"Ali," he murmured and she recognised the dangerous

tone of his voice as the same one that had whispered in her ear at *The Hummingbird*. "We're still supposed to be dating right?" He kept his voice pitched low, despite the saleswoman leaving as soon as he had stood up and walked over to her.

"Yes," she said and made herself ask the next question. "Why?"

"My friends know what I'm like—that if I want something, I'm all in."

"Okay," she said hesitantly and he continued as he took a singular step toward her.

"Blake for instance, knows that I don't hesitate to go after what I want."

"Right," she tried again, trying to see where this was going as he took two steps closer.

"And what I want right now..." Another step. "Is to taste you on my tongue as you come on my mouth."

Her chest heaved as she sucked in a breath. She wished she could say it was shock and not the thrill of what he'd said that had made her gasp, but it would have been a lie. And she'd never been good at telling those.

"So my question is," he whispered as he came to stand directly in front of her, his lips nearly brushing her own, "wouldn't it be suspicious to not do exactly that?"

She tilted her chin up slightly, as if daring him to kiss her, and his nostrils flared. "I guess you might be right." Would he really make good on his promise? Surely not.

"Sorry, ma'am," he called and Ali blinked, her mouth falling open as the saleswoman approached with a smile.

"How are we getting on over here?"

"We'll take the dress," he said, glancing back at her for her nod of approval before continuing, "and the store, for an hour." Christopher paused and licked his lips, "Actually, better make it two."

Two hours? What was he going to do for two hours? That seemed... excessive. Besides, there was no way this woman was going to agree.

"I'm sorry sir, I'm not sure I understand."

There. Ali smirked slightly, glad to be proven right, even if a stab of disappointment did run through her.

He reached inside his jacket pocket and pulled out a wad of bills while she gaped. Why the hell would he carry that kind of cash around? That was *not* normal.

He caught her look and raised an eyebrow. "Emergencies," he said, and the way his eyes sparkled made it clear exactly what he considered to fall under that purview. "I would like to rent the store for two hours so we can... try on more dresses." He handed her the wad of bills as the woman stood there disbelievingly, eyes wide and mouth slightly parted. "There should be around ten thousand there. Will that be enough?" He shook his head as if answering his own question before pulling out a smaller stack. "Here's an extra five, for the dress."

"Is this a joke?" the woman said faintly and he frowned before shaking his head. "Um, okay. Sure. I-I'll be back in a couple of hours then?"

"Perfect, thanks so much." He smiled at her as he strode away and flipped the sign on the door to *closed,* locking it as she slipped out the back.

Ali felt nearly as dazed as the saleswoman had looked as Christopher turned to her. What had just happened?

"Now, where were we? Right, I was going to pull this gorgeous dress off of you." He stopped mid-stride and tilted his head to one side. "Actually... let's leave it on."

Oh god... She knew her face must nearly be as red as her hair, but there was no doubt in her mind that she wanted this, flimsy as their excuse may have been.

His hands on her waist seemed to sear her skin even through the fabric of the dress, like his touch had branded her, claimed her.

He traced his hands down past the ruffle of material and smoothed them over the curve of her hips, following the line of her body as he sank to his knees. The bottom of the dress was form-fitting and he tsked as he tried to shimmy the hem up and failed.

"I'm sorry, gorgeous, but the dress has got to go." He didn't sound sorry at all as she turned for him and he eased the zipper down, inch by inch, deliberately slowly as if he was teasing himself as well as her.

The material pooled on the floor and he stepped in close behind her, the sensation of his suit jacket against her bare skin sending a thrill through her and heat pooling low in her stomach.

"Turn around," he murmured silkily and she obeyed, her arms twitching as she ignored her initial impulse to cover the bare, freckled skin of her chest.

His eyes darkened as his lips parted, a small breath escaping him that sounded a lot like a groan. "Tell me I can touch you."

Her mouth opened but she hesitated, remembering what he'd told her before about enjoying bossy women in bed. "Touch me, Christopher. Here," she commanded, cupping one breast in her hand and massaging it slightly, pinching the nipple between her thumb and the edge of her index finger.

He was coming undone before her eyes and she wasn't sure she'd ever seen anything sexier than a man as powerful, as in control, as Christopher surrendering to her. "Yes, ma'am."

His hand replaced her own, easily holding all of her as he imitated her movements before looking up at her for approval.

"Good boy," she said, slightly breathless and watched in fascination as a flush spread over the tops of his cheekbones. He kept up the torturous motion of his hand, sending sparks across her skin, and she wondered for a moment why he did nothing more. But when he glanced up at her again, she realized he was waiting for her direction.

"Now here," she said hoarsely, touching her pussy with one hand over her underwear and shuddering when his left hand covered her own, rotating slightly to ease the pressure building but not enough to fulfill her desire completely.

He hooked one finger into the thin band of her underwear and raised an eyebrow at her. She nodded. "Take them off."

He did as she asked and she stepped out of them once

they landed at her feet, bringing her bare chest to his crisp shirt.

Her boss' hand moved back to cover her but she shook her head. "Taste me," she said quietly and a wicked grin lit his face.

"With pleasure," he said, his words ghosting over the sensitive skin in front of him and making her breath catch. She hadn't shaved, but he didn't seem to mind—which was a good thing, because she didn't intend to do more than her usual trim to keep things neat and tidy down there even if she did start dating someone again.

He placed a kiss just below her navel and the muscles there quivered as he teased a line of kisses towards the peak of her pussy and parted her to place his mouth over her clit.

Her spine curved as she gasped and she felt him smile against her before he kissed her again and began to alternate between hot, hard kisses and long licks that had her panting with need. He didn't taste her like someone performing a perfunctory duty, no. He feasted like the taste of her was driving him wild, his tongue circling and flicking like it was an art he wanted to spend time perfecting, learning the way she moved.

She parted her legs even more, giving him easier access and he thanked her by dipping his tongue inside her pussy and pulsing it against her g-spot. He'd found it without any issues or hesitation and she had to admire that he was clearly a man who made prioritizing a woman's pleasure a necessity.

"Yes," she gasped as his mouth closed over her clit

while his tongue lapped at her entrance, tasting her wetness and pressing closer like he couldn't get enough. "Don't stop. *Fuck*, Christopher. Don't stop." Her voice had become desperate and when he guided her legs wider with a hand on her inner thigh, she didn't protest. He angled his head higher and reached his hands behind her to cup her ass as he pushed her forward until she was sitting on his face while he kneeled between her legs.

"I've got you," he said, pulling away for just a second to reassure her. "Relax."

His arms cradled her back, supporting her as he put his lips to her pussy again, torturing her clit with his mouth until she wasn't sure she could take any more. But he kept going, making her legs shake as his tongue pushed into her pussy and fucked her to a messy orgasm. She expected that to be the end, that he'd get up and wipe his face and they would leave, but he didn't move.

"What are you doing?" she said, voice rough from how loud she'd been moaning for him.

Christopher pressed small kisses to the outside of her pussy, making her clit pulse as his words blew warmth over it. "You didn't think I was done did you?"

"But... I already came."

"You think I'm satisfied with just one orgasm? Oh Alison," he licked a long line of heat from her clit to her entrance. "At least three is the standard. I want to feel you cream on my tongue, and your legs shake so hard you clamp them around my head. I want to ruin you for anyone else, in the best way possible. By my count," he said, checking his watch, "I've still got another forty-five minutes here with you. I should have asked for three hours, but I think I can make it work."

He stood and she nearly stumbled as her legs tried to remember how to function. He caught her around the waist and turned her so she could see her reflection in the mirror inside the opening dressing room opposite them. Her back was to his front and she could feel how hard he was against her ass but he tutted as she ground back against him.

"This is about you," he said, cupping her breasts with his hands and pinching the nipples to the point of pain as she watched him move in the mirror. His hands slid lower, cupping her hips as he smirked at her watching him in the reflection. "Do you want to watch me fuck you like this, Ali?"

Her hips twitched and his smirk deepened.

"Your wish..." He moved his right hand over her pussy, spreading her lips with two fingers as he slid his middle digit down to stroke her clit. "Is my command."

She leaned back against him as she watched him stroke her, her clit already pulsing from the over-sensitisation of her first orgasm. She looked away, not sure she would last if she kept watching him pleasuring her, but his free hand reached up to gently direct her jaw back so she couldn't look away.

One finger slid inside of her and the sound he made in her ear made her clench around him before he added a second finger. Her eyes were glazed with lust and her cheeks were pink as Christopher thrust his fingers into her quicker, filling the air around them with the sound and scent of her arousal just as she came for him again.

"Two," he reminded her, the cockiness on his face turning her on more if she was being honest with herself. He adjusted his cock, protruding from his trousers in a way that seemed painful, before he led her over to the bevy of small chairs where he'd been waiting when she'd come out of the dressing room.

She watched, confused, as he pushed them all together and then laid down against them with his knees bent so his legs still touched the floor.

"Come here," he urged and she walked forward to stand next to him. "Do you want to ride me?"

At first she thought he meant his cock, but when he helped her up and over his face, she understood what he meant.

"Are you sure? What if I suffocate you?" she said, hesitantly spreading her legs wider as he gazed up, hungrily.

"Then I'll die a happy man." His hands cupped her ass as he pressed her down onto his face and she gasped at the pressure, the wetness, the new friction. Her hips rocked instinctively and he moaned in approval, sucking on her clit until she cried out for him. This was something she'd never done before and he was right, annoyingly, he might have ruined her for anyone else.

Christopher moved his mouth in time with the steady writhing of her hips, plunging his tongue inside of her and flicking it until another flood of wetness made her hips quicken.

"Christopher," she warned, her words more of a pant than anything intelligible but he seemed to understand all the same. His arms wrapped around her tightly as he pressed her down firmly and she ground her pussy against his mouth, sensation completely taking over.

"Oh, oh, oh," she chanted as the waiting area chairs creaked under the motions of her frantic movements.

His tongue suddenly hit her clit at exactly the right angle and she exploded, her body tightening and shuddering as pulses of pleasure made her pussy flutter against his mouth until she slumped against him.

He stroked a hand down her back as she caught her breath before sitting up to look at him.

He was a mess, his mouth and nose were wet and glistening and his hair was tangled from where she'd fisted her hands in it. There was a lazy smile on his lips, like he was the one who'd been well-fucked instead of her.

"Look at that," he murmured, "ten minutes to spare."

Chapter Twenty

"You seem relaxed," Freya said off-handedly as she flicked through a magazine while Jesse cooked them all dinner—the one dish she knew how to make, a vegetarian spaghetti bolognese.

"Um, I guess," Ali said, knowing her voice sounded too high and strange, earning curious looks from her roommates as they peered at her.

"Oh my god," Jesse said, flinging down the wooden spoon she'd been using to stir the sauce and sending tomato everywhere. "You did it again."

Freya raised her eyebrows and Ali bit back a groan. "Okay fine, yes. But I'm only giving you details because it was... I don't know. I just need to check if sex was always supposed to be like this and I just didn't know it."

She told them about the encounter in the dress store and her roommates listened with rapt attention, leaning forward with wide eyes the longer she spoke.

"Just to clarify," Jesse said thoughtfully, "he's got you

off more than twice now and not asked for anything in return?"

"Yep."

Jesse shot Freya a look and she nodded in return.

"What?"

"Nothing. It's just I, for one, am impressed with your boldness and with his apparent skill."

She flushed at Jesse's words, remembering exactly how skillful Christopher had been. "So? Is this normal and I've just been doing it wrong all this time?"

"Yes," Jesse said at the same moment Freya said, "No."

Ali rolled her eyes. "You guys are so helpful."

"Look," Freya said, uncharacteristically sharp. "Clearly you like him. He obviously likes you. The sex is good. What's the problem?"

Jesse looked at Freya out of the corner of her eye and Ali couldn't help but agree. What was up with her?

"Well, he's my boss for one."

"If that was really an issue you wouldn't have been riding him like a rodeo bull in the middle of a shopping mall," Freya said and then turned back to her magazine with a sniff while we gaped at her.

"Okay," Jesse said at last, "who pissed in your coffee?"

She sighed as she set the magazine down. "I'm sorry, okay? It's just hard watching you make up excuses not to be happy, Ali. Some people would kill to have someone look at them the way Christopher looks at you."

"Are your parents putting pressure on you again?" Ali asked softly and Freya bit her lip and nodded.

"I don't want to marry just for the sake of it. I want to

find somebody I love. They don't seem to think love should play into it."

"Well, they're wrong," Jesse announced before cursing as the water for the pasta began to bubble over. "Tell them to fuck off."

Freya snorted. "I'll get right on that."

Jesse focused back on trying to salvage dinner and Ali leaned in closer to Freya. "You really think I should just go for it with Christopher?"

"I do," she nodded emphatically. "What's the worst that could happen?"

"I fall for him and he breaks my heart," Ali said, only half-joking. "Besides, maybe he's only in it for the sex."

"I know some guys love to give, but generally they want to come too. So if it was just for the sex..." Freya looked at her meaningfully and she sighed.

"I just..."

"Don't know how to trust anyone again after Jared?"

"Yeah," she admitted, looking away so she didn't have to see the pity on her face. "How does he look at me? Christopher, I mean." She'd always avoided the topic or rolled her eyes when her roommates had mentioned it before, but now she found that she actually wanted to know how it seemed to them from an outsider's perspective.

"Like he'd fuck up anyone who hurt you and still sleep like a baby after," Jesse said, clearly having heard her question and Freya half-shrugged, half-nodded.

"Not quite what I was going to say but not untrue," she allowed.

"Then what were you going to say?"

Freya paused as if considering her words carefully. "He looks at you like he's scared."

Ali reeled back. "Scared?"

"Not of you, but for you. The kind of fear you feel when someone you love is talking about doing something stupid, the worry that you'll lose them before you've really had them. He looks at you like you're holding his heart in your palm and seconds away from crushing it."

The silence was loud, only interrupted by the faint bubbling of the food on the stove.

"Damn," Jesse said and Ali was glad she had spoken first. "You know, you have a very poetic mind, Frey."

Her lips twitched. "Thank you."

It definitely gave Ali something to think about, especially when she remembered the conversation she'd overheard in Christopher's car with Denver. Maybe whatever this was between them, she just had to leap and hope he caught her before she hit the ground. She had been too sleepy on the way home for them to have any tension between them, but how would she feel when she saw him tomorrow?

Jesse turned off the stove and clattered around, grabbing bowls, before she placed the food down on the table. Surprisingly, it looked good.

The eggplant was garlicky and a perfect golden brown, and the pasta was only slightly overdone.

Jesse smiled when they didn't speak, just munched happily after thanking her for dinner.

"Do you want to see the dress?" Ali asked after their bowls were nearly cleared.

"The dress that closed an entire store?"

"The dress that led to, quote, *the best head of your life?*"

She glared at her two friends until they all burst out laughing. "Is that a yes?"

"Fine, fine, show us the sex dress."

She wrinkled her nose. "It's not a—"

Jesse waved her off as Freya tried not to snort pasta out of her nose.

Ali pushed away from the table and crossed the communal space to her room, slipping the dress out of its garment bag and carefully pulling it on. It was probably the most expensive piece of clothing she owned, but at least it was versatile enough to be worn for different occasions.

She stepped out of her bedroom and Jesse hooted as Freya's eyes went wide.

"Damn, no wonder you sent the man to his knees."

"You like?" She gave a little twirl and beamed when they both nodded and cooed over her.

"You look beautiful, Ali," Freya said and Ali smiled.

"I wish you guys could come to this thing."

"You'll be fine." Freya carefully set her cutlery down as Jesse wrinkled her nose.

"The magic of the dress is almost enough to make me go, but not quite," Jesse said and Ali sighed.

"It's okay, I'm just worried that I'll seem out of place."

Freya shook her head. "You'll be with Christopher, but even if you weren't it would be okay. Just own it. They will probably stare, they might even whisper, but who gives a fuck?" she finished, sounding eerily like Jesse who grinned and gave her a high-five before turning to Ali.

"Yeah, what she said."

Ali laughed and wished she could steal a little of their confidence, but she would just have to work out how to find her own and pretend like she belonged in that world, with Christopher on her arm, in the meantime.

Chapter Twenty-One

"Are you ready for tonight?"

She'd been chasing up some paperwork at Cassie's desk when Christopher approached, his low voice making her shiver. "Well, I do have the perfect dress," she teased and was pleased when his eyes turned molten.

A giggle came from a couple desks down and she tried not to grimace. They'd been the talk of the office for a couple of weeks now, and she'd quickly found that it was impossible to go anywhere without one of the girls asking if Christopher was a good kisser or one of the guys suddenly trying to ask her out now that she was unavailable. It was... odd. Like being in high school and sitting with the popular kids.

"I can pick you up from your place," Christopher said, either not caring or not noticing the looks they were drawing.

"That would be perfect." She smiled at him and her

breath caught in her chest when he leaned in and pressed a lingering kiss to her cheek before striding away.

She stared after him and then frowned when she caught people watching her intently. God, they were going to be incorrigible now.

HER SHOES WERE PINCHING her feet, but she'd never felt more beautiful. Friday had come around quicker than she could have imagined and Freya had insisted on helping with her hair and make-up that night. Ali had acquiesced fairly easily, Freya was much better with that sort of thing than she was. The only item of makeup she'd mastered was the winged liner she wore nearly every day—she could have her eyes done in under five minutes and matching wings to boot.

But for Rose and David's engagement party, she wanted a more understated look and Freya had done an amazing job, adding some kind of shimmer to her face that highlighted her cheekbones and made her look pleasantly sun-kissed.

Christopher had knocked on her door at ten-to-eight and her friends had watched them leave, peering around the corner of the door like overeager parents.

David was hosting the party at his manor house—which was really just a civilized way of saying mansion—that sat out of town and on a private patch of land. The gates had opened for Christopher's car automatically and gravel had crunched under her feet when she'd stepped out and wobbled, catching herself against the warm chest of her date with a gasp of surprise.

Christopher shot her a smile full of dry humor. "I was coming around to help you out of the car."

She laughed nervously as she stared past him and up at the property. Twinkling lights were wrapped around an archway of roses just before the front door and their sweet fragrance settled her nerves as she inhaled deeply and let out a long breath.

"Okay, I'm ready." They passed through the archway and a tall man behind the door, visible through the glass on either side, opened it for them.

He gave a cursory look inside their bags and nodded for them to go in. It would have seemed extreme if not for the very-real stalker who had shot and nearly killed both David and Rose just about a year ago. She had to imagine that the man on the door was also checking for known members of the press too as this event, much like the upcoming wedding retreat, was a media blackout zone.

The unmistakable sound of chatter, music and laughter was coming from straight ahead of them as they made their way deeper into the house and, despite the horrors that had occurred there not so long ago, she couldn't help but admire the woodwork and art that made up David Blake's home.

Christopher led them into a ballroom where a band was set up and several heads turned as they moved through the door, but Ali was too busy musing over the fact that David had an actual *ballroom* in his house to notice whether the stares were curious, appreciative, or openly hostile.

More sparkly lights hung from the walls, cascading in sheets that made the bride-to-be glow as she swayed her way over to them with her fiance on her arm.

"Christopher!" she pressed a kiss to his cheek and then pulled back to look at Ali.

"Alison! It's good to see you again."

"You too," she said and Rose smiled, looking like an angel in her shimmery silver dress.

"You work at *Horizons,* right?"

"I'm Christopher's assistant," she confirmed and was surprised by the teasing look Rose shot her boss.

"Very naughty of you Christopher. Can you believe it, Blake? Our goody-two-shoes breaking the rules?"

Christopher shrugged. "It's not against the rules. I checked."

David snorted as he reached out and shook his best friend and business partner's hand. "Of course you did. Nice to see you again, Ali."

"It's gorgeous in here," she said, which earned her a pleased look from David and a beaming smile from Rose.

"Thank you! My friend Maia helped us decorate. Anyway, go and get a drink, dance, we'll catch up with you later."

Christopher pressed a kiss to Rose's cheek as they passed and Ali glanced back to see David folding Rose into a slow dance despite the up-tempo song.

"They're sweet together."

Christopher snorted. "You might be the only person to

ever say that—though it's true that they've mellowed out a lot."

Ali raised an eyebrow but didn't question him further as he passed a flute of champagne to her and she took a sip.

"You look stunning, by the way," he said, leaning down to murmur into her ear and she smiled as she sipped her drink. "I may have to fight one or two guys tonight to keep you."

"You clean up well yourself," she teased, though truthfully he looked similar to the way he always did, with the addition of a little more gel in his hair and a suit that probably cost more than her entire apartment.

Her smile faded as she remembered what they were there to do, and that it would mean betraying the couple who had greeted them with open arms just moments ago.

Christopher seemed to sense the change in her mood, grabbing her glass out of her hand as he caught her eye. "Dance with me."

She didn't have the chance to accept or decline before he was sweeping her into his arms and every line of her body was set perfectly against his. Unlike David and Rose, Christopher didn't slow dance with her. No, he maneuvered her body expertly, waltzing her around like it was effortless as she did her best not to step on his feet.

People were staring, and she nearly stumbled when one particularly sour gaze seemed to stare daggers at her.

"Relax," he murmured as the band shifted into an acoustic version of *Eternal Flame* and he somehow moved impossibly closer. His cologne was intoxicating and she swallowed hard when she looked up and found his lips just a breath away from hers, his nose grazing her skin, his breath smelling like champagne and desire.

"I'm sorry," she said quietly as the lead singer's guitar offered them a moment of relative privacy despite the other bodies swaying around them in time to the music. "For putting you in this position."

He shook his head. "It was my choice to make, not yours. You don't need to apologize to me. Not ever."

She didn't reply, just soaked in the feeling of him pressed against her, like he was trying to sink into her skin.

The song ended and they broke apart, leaving her feeling cold as they blended with the moving crowd and tried to head back toward the door that led to the rest of the house. They were waylaid as several people wanted to stop and talk to Christopher and just as they managed to escape, David and Rose appeared again.

David smiled at her, his blue eyes looking especially bright against the silver of his tie and the streaks of gold in his dark blonde hair. "Can I steal your date for a dance, Chris?"

"You'll have to ask her," he said with a smirk. "She's the boss, you know."

She blushed slightly, knowing exactly what he was referring to, before accepting David's hand and letting him pull her out onto the dance floor.

"It's nice seeing him so happy," David said as they swayed back and forth while they watched Rose dance with Christopher. "He's wanted to ask you out for ages, you know," David said slyly and she laughed. "How did he finally get up the courage?"

"He rescued me from my ex," she said, deciding to give him as much honesty as she was able. "And then we went out to dinner."

"*The Hummingbird*," David said knowingly, "I saw that in the press. It's funny really, that's where Rose and I reconnected too."

"Must be something in the drinks over there."

They danced for just the one song and then David swept his bride back into his arms as they moved to the music again. A commotion sounded in the corner off to the left and a sea of heads turned as one of the servers dropped a platter of miniature food onto the floor.

"Come on," Christopher muttered and she followed him out of the room while the server apologized profusely. "I only paid them for a five-minute distraction."

She raised an eyebrow at him, wondering when he'd found the time to pull that off. "This place is massive," she muttered as they hurried up the main staircase and Christopher led them around a corner to a long corridor. Moonlight spilled in through a large window seat and they bypassed it entirely to stop outside of what looked like any other hardwood door.

"It used to be a dressing room," Christopher muttered, "but Blake redesigned it into an office for Rose last month."

As much as it pained her to have involved him, it was damn handy having someone on the inside.

They glanced up and down the corridor before turning the handle and stepping inside. There was a level of organization to the space that put even Ali's desk to shame. A hardwood desk spanned the back wall, overlooking the front drive, and thick, cream carpet covered the floor and made her nervous to walk on it with her heels on.

Ali slipped off her shoes, not wanting to leave mud or footprints on the carpet, but it felt like even more of an invasion to sink her toes into the plush softness.

Christopher hurried over to the desk and looked it over with a critical eye without touching anything, even going so far as to swat her hand away when Ali reached for a pile of papers.

"She'll know if you move anything," he said matter of factly and Ali grimaced, the thought sending shivers over her skin like Rose DuLoe was a bogeyman and not a savvy business woman and heiress.

He carefully slid open one of the drawers that lined the right side of the desk beneath the top and then they both froze as the sound of footsteps reached them from the other side of the office door.

They held still until the sound passed and then Christopher went back to opening drawers one by one while she watched uselessly, wringing her hands.

"Here," he said and she breathed a sigh of relief when he set the large, white binder on top of the desk. Inside were concept drawings of table placements, flowers, dresses, and even rings. Scraps of fabric had been pinned to the thick pages, as well as contact details for various designers and tailors. It was so much information it was dizzying—surely it wasn't the norm to put so much work into what was essentially a very fancy party? Or maybe it was in Rose's world and, she realized with a pang as she looked at the man beside her, Christopher's too. Though, to be fair to Rose, this wedding had been a bit of a whirlwind from the start—planning a wedding of this size in about eight months would be a feat for anyone, let alone a ceremony of this magnitude.

But since the security scare they'd had, they'd publicly come out and said they didn't want to waste any time—life was short. Of course, they'd only made the statement because the press had been going wild over the theory of a shotgun wedding because of a DuBlake baby.

Ali shook her head, trying to re-focus back on their task. More footsteps thudded past outside and she didn't realize she'd held her breath until she started to feel lightheaded.

"Let's get a few pictures and get back to the party," Christopher said quietly and she nodded, pulling out her phone and hovering it over the pages detailing the potential flavors of cake and the bakery Rose had settled on.

Flash.

Ali froze. *Crap.* She hadn't expected that to be so bright.

"Hurry," Christopher muttered, peering out of the window to see if anyone had spotted the flare of light. Ali snapped a few more pictures and then they moved back across the carpet to the door, picking up her shoes as they went.

Christopher eased the door shut behind them and Ali slid on her heels

Quickened footsteps headed their way and she froze,

staring up at Christopher with big eyes. Someone had seen her camera flash after all.

The sound moved closer to them, clearly heading to Rose's office to investigate. They couldn't run without being heard and caught, they couldn't hide in the long stretch of corridor and the only other room was closer to the stairs than they currently were. They were trapped.

Christopher had clearly come to the same conclusion, and as the guard's shadow appeared on the floor, he pushed her against the wall, sank his hands into her hair, and crashed his lips to hers.

It occurred to her then how absurd it was that this was their first kiss, that he'd tasted her and teased her, all without ever committing to this one last unraveling. And she thought she knew why, because she had never moved to cross that line either. Sex was one thing—kissing, affection, tenderness, was another, and this was exactly like that. It was ferocity packaged as a kiss that threatened to break her, like he was the waves the shore drowned for, happily.

Her hands pulled him closer, desperate for more, his tongue against hers wringing a gasp from her lips that felt like it had been squeezed from her soul, like she'd been walking around with only half of herself without realizing it until his mouth sealed itself to hers.

I want to ruin you for anyone else. That was what he'd told her before, and as the wall dug into her back and a throat cleared somewhere beyond her, she knew he'd lived up to that promise. Her mouth was still puffy from his kisses, her chest heaving as he pulled away to look at the security officer standing just six feet away and smirked.

"A little privacy?"

The guard shifted awkwardly but didn't back down as Ali tried to get a hold of herself.

"I'm sorry sir, but this part of the house is off-limits to guests."

"I'm the groom's best friend," Christopher said, cocking an eyebrow with more arrogance than she'd ever seen him wield before and she was surprised by how much it turned her on.

Recognition lit in the man's eyes and he nodded. "Ah. Sorry to have disturbed you."

Christopher grinned like he'd just been caught making out in the middle of his friend's party—which, for all the guard knew, was true. "No worries. Hey, you might want to tell that other guy the same thing though. I didn't recognise him and he was gone before I could try and talk to him."

"Other guy?" the guard said, instantly stiffening and looking alert as Ali tried not to let her confusion show.

"Yeah, tall, skinny guy with brown hair, maybe? He ran off in that direction." Christopher gestured behind them and the guard nodded before setting off at a brisk pace.

Silence fell between them as the guard's form retreated. It didn't escape her notice that the vague description he'd told the guard could have matched Jared —he was thinking two steps ahead as always.

The amount of security shouldn't have been a surprise,

clearly Rose and David were struggling to reclaim their peace after being stalked and attacked, and Ali could tell that violating that privacy had hurt Christopher ten times more than it had her. They were his friends after all, and he was betraying them for her. There was nothing she could really say about that to make him feel better, so instead she reached up to wipe away the smear of lipstick from his mouth and folded her arm into his as they made their way back downstairs to the party that raged on below.

Chapter Twenty-Two

As soon as she'd gotten home last night, she'd sent Jared all the photos she'd managed to take of the guests along with what they'd found in Rose's office. It had made her feel dirty, going into someone's home and using them the way she had, but if she wanted to keep her mother safe and her own name out of the press it was necessary. She needed to reclaim some peace, some normality, and so she headed to the park for the yoga class that ran there.

It was relatively cool out but the setting sun was warm, and as they stretched in the sunlight she could feel some of her tension draining away. This was what she needed, to focus on herself and her body's movements rather than the way she felt for her boss, her worry for her mom, or any other plethora of things overshadowing her life recently.

She liked this class specifically because it was small and the instructor was soothing. Whenever she finished she always thought that she should do it more often—not that she actually followed up on it.

They did their cool down stretches and Ali waved goodbye to the instructor as she began the walk home, debating whether or not she should stop and detour to *Lola's* for a coffee.

"Did I not make myself clear about the consequences of your failure?"

Her muscles tensed and she faltered with one foot in the air, caught between steps. Jared. She spun around and found him behind her. A cap on his head obscured his face from any passersby, but she was close enough to see the dark circles and bloodshot quality of his eyes, as well as the strange way he kept twitching even as he stood still. "I don't know what you're talking about. I sent you everything I had," she said carefully and then gave a surreptitious glance around to see if anyone from the class was close. Nothing. It was just them.

"You sent me twenty photos, half of which were too blurry to do anything with, and the only info you got from that book was who was making their wedding cake."

"Well, that's good right? A reveal?" she tried and jumped when he cursed, throwing a hand out in agitation and nearly catching her across the cheek.

"Dumb bitch. They were papped leaving that bakery weeks ago! You gave me nothing."

Her heart began to beat so fast it made her feel sick. "Well, what about the photos of the guests?"

"Useless," he grunted. "The majority of them posted on

their socials that they were attending and who they were wearing. You've disappointed me, Alison."

"I didn't mean to—I tried my best and—"

"Your best isn't good enough. What am I supposed to do with the shit you sent me? Are you still trying to stall me like before? Because I promise I won't let you off so easily this time and it won't just be you who pays the price." He was panting and spittle flew as he yelled, making her shy back.

Mouth running dry, she croaked out, "No! Look, I'm sorry I'm not a professional photographer, okay? I did what I could."

He watched her with a strange vacant look in his eyes and when he stepped toward her she stumbled back. "The consequences," he said softly, "are on you. Maybe it will help motivate you to *try* a little harder next time."

She didn't know what else to say and he seemed to be done talking, shoving his way past her without another word, his shoulder knocking into her so hard that she knew she'd have a bruise.

He'd seemed more unhinged than usual, and it made her wonder what exactly he was mixed up in to need the money from the photos so badly. Then there were the drugs he'd somehow managed to have planted... It all added up to a worrying picture—worse, he'd managed to drag her and Christopher into his mess too. She hurried home, anxious about what she might find when she got there. Any semblance of calm had been stripped away as her brain worked to conjure up the worst-case scenarios possible. She paced back and forth in her apartment as her breaths left her in rasps that bordered on a wheeze and she didn't know what to do. What had he meant when he said the consequences were on her? What was he planning?

She wasn't sure how much time had passed since she'd seen him, but her legs ached from pacing so vigorously and her jaw hurt from clenching it. Dark spots danced in her vision and she knew she needed help when she sank to the ground and couldn't move.

Her fingers felt numb as she scrolled through her contacts for Christopher's number. Everything felt far away as it rang in her ear and Christopher's voice seemed tinny when he answered. "Hello? Ali?"

She couldn't seem to get her voice to work or her lips to move as fear kept her paralyzed. Was Jared going to hurt her? Or her mother?

"Are you at home?" She heard Christopher ask faintly and she managed to get just one word past her chattering teeth.

"Yes."

"Stay there. I'm coming."

The phone slipped from fingers that felt stiff with cold and she barely noticed as it thumped to her living room floor.

What could Jared be doing right at that moment? What if he was on his way to her place right then? What if he got to her before Christopher did?

She fell when she tried to stand and staggered into the chairs surrounding the dining table before she managed to get past them and into the kitchen. At least Freya and

Jesse were both out, Jared wouldn't be able to hurt them if he came for her.

All of her memories of him smiling and laughing with her were now overlaid by the smug smirk on his face when he'd looked up at the video recording, and the calm with which he'd said he'd hurt her at the burger joint. He'd seemed strung out when he'd confronted her on the way home, but she'd never seen him like that before or seen him doing drugs when they were together.

She grabbed one of the biggest knives in the kitchen she could find and hurried to her bedroom. She needed to call her mom.

The phone rang for what seemed like forever, Ali's breaths sounding back at her through the white noise of phone static until it picked up with a click.

"Mom?"

"Oh hey, kiddo. I was actually just about to call you—"

"Mom, you need to listen to me. Take Caleb and get out of town. Just for tonight, okay?"

There was a pause and then she said slowly, "I'm already out of town, honey. I had tickets to the show in Richmond, remember?"

A tear dripped down her face as relief overwhelmed her. "Okay, good. That's good. I-I have to go. I'll call you later okay?"

"Wait, Alison—"

She hung up and then jumped at a thump at the front door. The lamp in her room was on low, so she closed the door and crept out into the darkness of the living area, crouching down by the sofa to peer at the door as someone tried the handle.

Her fingers curled tightly around the hilt of the knife until she felt sure she would have the imprint of it etched into her palm forever. The door rattled as someone pounded on it.

Surely Jared wouldn't knock?

"Ali? Are you okay?"

The knife clattered to the ground as she ran to the door and unlocked it, flinging it wide and then swaying when she saw Christopher standing on the threshold.

"You came," she whispered and he reached for her as soon as he stepped inside the apartment.

"Of course I did. I will always come when you call, Alison."

Her body shuddered as she let her guard down and Christopher held her up, cradling her to his chest and pushing his fingers through her hair before he reached out to close her front door behind them and lock it.

"Everything's okay," he murmured, "you're safe."

"I'm sorry I called you," she mumbled, comforted by his heartbeat beneath her ear. "I shouldn't have put you at risk too."

He gently eased her away from him and cupped her jaw, his deep brown eyes peering at her with concern. "What do you mean?"

She opened her mouth to explain but then her phone rang and a strange sense that something was wrong made her rush to get it.

"Freya?" she said as she answered. "Are you alright?"

"I'm okay, but Ali, I just got a call from Caleb." No. *No.* She'd just spoken to her mom and she'd been fine. "They got a call from your mom's neighbor, June? Your mom's place... Well, it's on fire. He said you hung up on your mom before she could tell you."

On fire. On *fire?* She had been silent for too long because Freya prompted her, the worry in her voice translating fine over the phone.

"Ali? I'm sorry. But they're both fine, apparently they were out of town."

"I know," she said, voice cracking, so she cleared her throat and repeated herself. "Thanks for letting me know, Frey."

"Of course. Are you going to be okay? Do you need me to come home?"

Ali glanced back to find Christopher sitting on their couch, watching her. "It's fine, Christopher's here with me."

She hung up after promising Freya she'd call if she needed her and then flopped onto the couch next to her boss.

"Someone set my mom's house on fire," she said and Christopher breathed a curse. "She's fine, she was away for the weekend. But I need to get her out of here, somewhere safe."

"And what about you?"

She followed the direction of his gaze and picked up the knife from the floor, dropping it onto the fuzzy table-chair. "I'll be okay."

He pushed a hand through his hair and it was then that she noticed what he was wearing.

"Were you asleep when I called?"

A blush colored his cheeks as he glanced down at the pajama pants and mismatched shoes on his feet. "No, I was just relaxing. I, um, tried to get here as fast as I could—it's just lucky there's not much traffic at this time coming into the city."

"Well, thank you for coming," she said and felt like she should probably let him go back to his evening even as she desperately wanted him to stay. And not just because Jared had scared her shitless.

No, she couldn't get the kiss they'd shared the night before out of her head, like it was haunting her.

"Ali..."

She couldn't meet his eyes and when she heard him sigh, she figured he was leaving. A soft touch to her shoulder made her head jerk up in surprise. "It's okay to ask for help sometimes, you know. It's okay to need it."

There was a lump in her throat that wouldn't fade no matter how much she swallowed, so she nodded slightly and he moved closer. He smelled like wood smoke and the outdoors, and she couldn't help but relax slightly.

Two fingers tilted her chin up and her heart caught in her throat as his lips brushed hers lightly, sending a shockwave through her system.

"Come home with me," he murmured against her mouth, and she didn't know what she'd been expecting him to say but it hadn't been that. "I don't like the thought of you being here by yourself. The wedding's not that far away now, so why don't you come and stay with me until this is all figured out? I promise I'll keep you safe."

His face was open and earnest and his thumb was stroking tiny circles into her palm that made all her muscles feel like goo.

"I'm scared," she admitted and he pressed a kiss to her forehead.

"I know. This.. what *he* did tonight changes things."

"Do you think maybe Denver could try hacking him again? See if we can prove he was at my mom's when the fire was set?"

Christopher bit his lip and nodded slowly. "We can try. You think he did it himself?"

She shrugged. "It's the best shot we have at getting the cops to do something at this point. And he never really introduced me to any of his friends, now that I think about it. I guess I'd just assumed he didn't have any."

"Strange, he seemed like such a nice guy," Christopher quipped and she snorted.

"Okay. If you're sure you want me there—"

"I do," he said quickly and she could feel herself blushing.

"Okay then. I'll just... grab a few things."

He nodded and stayed standing where he was while she grabbed some clothes and toiletries and shoved them all into an overnight bag she'd forgotten she owned and had found at the back of her wardrobe.

"Ready?" he asked about ten minutes later and she nodded, feeling nervous but in a good way, like this could change everything.

"I already called Denver while you were packing," he said as they walked out of her door and headed out of her building to the haphazard parking job he'd performed when he'd rushed in to see her. "He's going to see what he can find. We're going to get him, Ali. He will pay for all of this."

She climbed into the car while he placed her bag in the back. She hoped he was right, but more than anything she hoped that they caught up to her ex before he decided to come looking for them next.

Chapter Twenty-Three

Christopher's place was nothing like she was expecting. She wasn't sure what, exactly, she'd been imagining this whole time—maybe something sleek and modern, similar to the style of the office in the city, but this was the opposite of that. It was quiet, tucked away like a small slice of heaven in an otherwise urban jungle.

The drive had been relatively quick, but she could see how it would likely take a lot longer during rush hour. But even with the added commute time, this summer house was worth it.

He pulled into a turning that was nearly obscured by the thick canopy of greenery that overshadowed the road, and it was clear from how easily he managed the turn in the dark that this was routine for him.

The house was smaller than she would have expected, especially so soon after seeing David Blake's house—Christopher also came from old money, so she had no doubt he could likely afford something similar. That told her he'd gone for this comparatively modest home because he liked it and she found herself fixating on that detail as he turned off the engine and they got out of the car. Maybe it was because it made her feel that they weren't from entirely different worlds after all. Common ground.

They were far enough out of the city that they could see the stars a little, and she smiled when she saw that several lights had been left on in Christopher's haste to get to her.

"It's lovely," she said and it honestly felt like the perfect word for the house. It was built from a mixture of stone and timber, making it feel like it could have sprouted from the ground, and a trellis of wildflowers ran up the side of the wall next to the door, leaving a sweet scent in her nose as he held the door open for her.

"Thank you," he replied as he closed and locked the door behind them. "It's kind of my retreat from the world."

A coat rack hung on the wall but was mostly empty other than an umbrella and a thick winter coat. The downstairs seemed to be split between a lounge and a kitchen diner that were opposite each other, the hall running between.

He was watching her and she squirmed uncomfortably, not sure whether to take off her shoes and just generally waiting for his direction.

"Make yourself at home," he said a moment later, like he'd read her mind, and she toed off her boots and placed them on the shoe rack underneath the coats.

A faint humming sound drifted to her and she realized

Christopher had gone on without her. She could see him through the gaps between the wooden beams and he looked like he was... making tea?

"Are you secretly British?" she teased as she walked into the kitchen and accepted the mug he handed her. "I don't think I've ever seen anyone with an actual kettle."

"Wait until you see my teapot collection," he mused and a small laugh left her.

The bottom half of the kitchen and lounge walls were solid, but she could see through the top of the open walls to the room opposite, separated by thick wooden beams.

"Come on," he said, noticing the direction of her gaze and leading her into the other room before nudging her into a tan leather armchair covered with blankets. It shouldn't have surprised her so much that a man who ran an interior design company—albeit for office spaces primarily—would have such good taste.

"Not what you were expecting, huh?" The smile on his face said he wasn't offended as he sat down on the chair next to hers, and she relaxed as she cupped the warm mug of tea. She was generally more of a coffee drinker, but it was hot and soothing as she blew on it and sipped.

"No," she admitted, "but I like it."

"I'm glad. I want you to feel comfortable here."

"Why?"

He stiffened, as if he hadn't even realized what he'd said, before taking a long gulp of tea and sputtering when it clearly burned his mouth. "How are you drinking yours already?"

She raised an eyebrow, ignoring his question as he avoided hers.

He sighed and set his cup down onto the light wood coffee table in the center of the room. "Maybe this makes me a fool. I know what we're doing... Well, you never wanted it. We were supposed to be pretending."

Supposed to be. Her mind seemed to skip and stop on those words like a record scratching to a halt.

"But I like you. I liked pretending you were mine and walking into that party with you on my arm, like you belonged there. I know it wasn't meant to be real, I do. But it was the most real thing I've felt for someone in what feels like forever."

Was she still breathing? She took in a ragged breath just in case and tried to swallow but her mouth was too dry. She sipped her tea but didn't look away from him. She had asked, hadn't she, and she couldn't say she was disappointed with the answer—not if she was being honest with herself anyway.

"Say something, please." He leaned forward so his elbows were on his knees and in the low light he looked even more devastating than usual. "If you want to leave, if I made you uncomfortable, just say the word and I'll take you home. Or wherever you want to go."

"You didn't," she said quickly, the words flying out of her so fast they blurred together. "I'm not uncomfortable."

"But you don't feel the same," he said, nodding like it was what he'd expected and she didn't know how he could have been so oblivious, so wrong.

"Christopher..."

"No, it's okay. You don't have to explain. I get it."

"Shut up," she said, exasperation making her voice breathless and he straightened in surprise. "It felt real to me too," she said, biting her lip.

"Thank God," he breathed and stood, crossing the space between them in one stride to sink one hand into her hair as his lips met hers.

Kissing Christopher felt natural, like breathing. Her skin tightened with electricity and her breaths came rapidly as they deepened the kiss. She would have let him strip her bare right then and there but he pulled away, eyes hooded and heavy and his lips red from the force of their kiss.

"Upstairs?"

She nodded and then squealed when he scooped her up into his arms and carried her with ease.

Thankfully, the stairs were few and the distance to the bedroom was short. He put her down once they were inside, sliding her down the length of his body so she could feel how much he wanted this—and she knew she felt the same.

"You're sure?" she murmured, needing to check one last time that this wasn't a fever dream brought on by her deepest desires. "No more pretending?"

He lifted her hand from her side and pressed her palm to the hard length of him straining against the material of his pants. "Does *this* feel pretend to you?" he said, groaning when her hand tightened on him, stroking him lightly. She was hungry for this, she realized. He had tasted her, touched her, but this was the first time he'd let her touch him in return.

"Why not before?" she asked and he seemed to know exactly what she meant.

"I couldn't let you touch me like that. Not when it would mean more to me than you."

"You never meant any less," she said, and meant it. "Let me show you." She bent her knees and knelt on the floor in front of him, lowering his pants with a smooth tug of her hand and feeling her mouth water when he fell free of the material.

"You don't know." she said huskily as she wrapped one hand around him, "how many times I've thought about this. Though I'll admit that in my head this happened while you were sitting at your desk."

He chuckled but the sound turned into a groan at the first touch of her mouth as she kissed her way from the base of his cock to its tip.

"Well," he said somewhat breathlessly, "I hope I can live up to the fantasy."

Ali didn't reply, too busy running her tongue over the underside of him and wrapping her mouth around his head, sucking him gently as she smoothed her tongue over his slit.

She took him deeper, dipping her head towards him in a rhythmic movement that quickened the more he twitched in her mouth.

"Ali," he said and then cursed. "Fuck. You need to stop. I'm not ready for this to end yet and if you keep going on like that..." His hips flexed as he pumped into her mouth and she hollowed her cheeks to suck him harder. They had all night, and she wanted to taste him on her tongue, to feel him lose control beneath her.

His hands fisted in her hair as she flicked her tongue over his tip and his head fell back with a gasp that set her blood aflame. "Ali, can I fuck your mouth?"

She moaned around him in response and he thrust forward until she gagged, but she let him in deeper as he rocked his hips.

"Look at you," he groaned and she raised her eyes to his as she swallowed him down. "You're taking it so well, Ali."

She backed up, paying close attention to his sensitive tip, before letting him thrust all the way back into her mouth. His pace sped up as he started to come undone, hands tightening in her hair and her name a prayer on his breath until he pulsed against her tongue and she felt his come hitting her throat.

She swallowed and licked his head for good measure before standing up and wiping her mouth.

His eyes were dazed when they opened and she laughed when he swayed. "That was... Thank you."

"It was a long time coming." She smirked and he pulled her close, pressing a kiss to her mouth and then her forehead.

"I'm going to need a little time to recover," he said and then her eyes widened, feasting on him eagerly as he lifted his tee over his head, revealing the cut of his abs and the broad shoulders she'd clung to while she'd rode his face in the department store. "But luckily my tongue and my fingers work just fine."

He reached for her top and made a noise of approval when he saw she was bare beneath it, before tugging down her pajama bottoms and smoothing a hand over her ass.

"Very lucky," she said with a smirk and opened eagerly for him when his lips teased hers, but he was just as desperate for her as she was for him and it felt good to be on equal footing.

"Bed, now." The deep rumble of his voice against her skin made her thighs squeeze together before she obeyed. The covers were plain white and the bed big enough that she could only just about touch each side with her fingertips when she spread out like a starfish. He chuckled watching her and tutted when she moved to bring her arms and legs back together.

"No, no, I was enjoying the view."

His body pressed hers down into the bed and the warmth from his skin made her arch against him appreciatively while he kissed down her neck, to the sensitive spot beneath her chin, and over her breasts.

He rolled one nipple between his fingers and watched her reaction keenly, learning what she enjoyed, how much pressure to apply to make her writhe for him.

The damp marks of his lips on her skin cooled in the air as he passed over her stomach and licked his way up her inner thighs with long kisses that had her eager for more.

One finger pushed between her legs as he stroked her clit and crooked his finger at her entrance. "So wet for me already, Ali."

The finger teasing her slid into her pussy knuckle deep

and he didn't move until she begged him, pushing her hips down on his hand and grinding desperately for some friction.

"More," she gasped and he obeyed, adding a second finger to the first and then leaning down to kneel between her legs.

She recognised the hunger on his face—it was how she'd felt when she'd finally tasted him. She smirked. "Matching up to your own fantasies?"

"Surpassing them," he said, bringing his mouth to the wetness gathering for him, "easily."

Her hips rose from the bed as he teased her with his tongue, running the tip along the edge of her clit until high, breathy sounds escaped from her lips and he grinned with smug satisfaction.

He pressed her legs wider, and the expression on his face made her feel like a particularly adored work of art—one he wouldn't ever tire of admiring. "Gorgeous," he said, leaning back to appreciate her sprawled on his bed before him. "I could do this all day," he mumbled against her skin as he resumed fucking her with his fingers and tongue.

He'd found exactly the right pressure and when his tongue flicked over her clit before he sucked on it mercilessly, she felt herself shatter as she cried out for him.

"I love the way you say my name," he panted as he propped himself up. "I think it's my favorite sound in the whole world. Especially when you scream it the way you did just then."

She couldn't reply, too busy trying to return to earth as

her heartbeat slowed, only to pick up again a moment later when he teased one finger through her wetness.

"Can you take more, Ali? Because I desperately want to watch as my cock fills that pretty pussy. I want to feel you tighten around me, feel your heat on my cock when you come."

Suddenly, she was wide awake. "Yes."

"You want that, Alison?" he said as he curled one finger inside her and she gasped. "Tell me how much."

"I want you," she groaned as he worked two more fingers inside of her, sliding in easily after he'd made her come the first time. "Now. Fuck me, Christopher."

The sound of his name proved to be his undoing as he cursed, pressing forward so he was lined up against her and shuddering as his head slicked through her come.

He paused. "Er, I realize this is bad timing, but... protection?"

She slumped, wanting so badly for him to just slide inside her. "I don't have any condoms on me. I have an IUD though."

"And with Jared...?"

She wrinkled her nose, not enjoying the reminder of her ex at that moment. "We used a condom. Always."

"I haven't slept with anyone for a long time," he admitted and chuckled at the surprise on her face. "I was clean the last time I got tested."

"Okay," she said and his eyes darkened as his cock twitched against her.

"Okay?"

"Now," she said desperately and he didn't hold back, tipping her thighs up with his hands as he filled her.

"Ali," he groaned, watching the space between them shrink as he sank all the way into her pussy before pulling away and thrusting back inside faster, little sparks of pleasure stemming from the dragging motion of his cock.

"Yes," she cried. "Fuck." She let her thighs fall wider, and he pushed in deeper as the wet sounds of their fucking filled the room alongside their gasps and moans for each other. "Christopher," she said as she raised her hips and he slid an arm under her back to grind himself against her fully, the base of his cock nudging at her clit and making her breathing quicken as she neared the edge.

He pulled away and she whimpered with need until he scooped her up and flipped her over, entering her again from behind her as he reached between them to stroke her clit.

The pressure was too much, and she could feel her walls clamping down around him as she came. He stroked her through the orgasm and didn't let up. She raised her body and entwined her arms around his neck as her back pressed to his chest.

The pump of his hips got harder as he rocked her on his cock, and the sensation of his fingers on her over-sensitised clit had her falling apart all over again as he finished inside her with her name on his lips.

She slumped back down onto the bed, and he dropped down beside her as they both caught their breath.

"The bathroom's just down the hall," he said once he could talk again, "if you want to pee or anything."

She smiled tiredly, knowing she should do exactly that but she was so exhausted and the bed was so soft.

"What are we doing about work this week?" she mumbled sleepily. It had to be at least four AM and if she didn't get her beauty sleep she would be in no condition to work anytime soon.

"We're working from home." He chuckled slightly and helped her sit up as they headed to the bathroom together. "I put a good word in with the boss."

She rolled her eyes but smiled as they pushed open the door. "HR will have a field day with that one."

Chapter Twenty-Four

The bed felt cozier than usual, and an unfamiliar warmth radiated from beside her. Ali's eyes fluttered open to find sunlight pouring into a room that wasn't hers and her boss asleep next to her.

They'd spent a long time talking last night, as well as doing other things that required use of their mouths, but she felt surprisingly refreshed. Maybe that was the result of a ridiculous amount of orgasms, or that the mattress that was literally to die for.

Or, she considered as she reached for her phone on the floor, it could be that it was well into the afternoon and she'd slept for just over eight hours.

The only thing that made her heart race was Jared's name on her screen, indicating that she had a message.

JARED: Just because I didn't come for you, doesn't mean I don't know where you are.

. . .

THERE WAS a video attached and a cold sweat broke out along her forehead as she hit play.

It was Christopher's living room, the lights from the kitchen illuminating two figures sitting and talking. One in an armchair, the other on the sofa opposite. Suddenly one of the figures stood and walked over to the other and—

Ali swallowed the bile that rose in her throat. Jared had been there last night. While Christopher had kissed her and brought her upstairs, her ex had been here. It was clearly shot from outside the house, perhaps the only comfort she had, but the fact that he kept being able to locate her like this was both infuriating and worrying.

"What's wrong?"

She wasn't sure how long Christopher had been awake, watching her, but he'd clearly seen the expression on her face and knew something was amiss.

"It's him," she said, nodding to the phone and the still image of Christopher bending down to kiss her in the armchair. "He was here last night."

"Bastard." He sat up in bed and the sheets puddled at his waist. "I'm so sorry Ali, I don't know he found you here."

She shook her head. "I think we should call Denver."

"I'll call," he said sternly. "You need to call your mom, make sure she's okay."

God. The fire. He was right. Caleb was taking good care of her mom, she was sure, but she still needed to talk to her herself and just hear her voice. She felt more than a little guilty that she hadn't called her back last night, but she hadn't had the mental capacity to comfort her when she'd been falling apart too.

"Sounds like a plan."

"You okay if I take the first shower?" he asked and she chuckled.

"It's your house."

"True," he acknowledged. "Does that mean I'm in charge, then?"

She laughed at the wicked gleam in his eyes. "Don't push your luck."

"You DIDN'T TELL me you booked my mom on a flight to Paris." She'd finished her call with her mom and had a quick enough shower to find Christopher still getting dressed after she walked into his room. "I was thinking about going to see her."

Christopher turned around, brows furrowed as he buttoned up his shirt. "I'm sorry, I didn't mean to overstep. I should have asked—"

"I'm not mad." She held up one hand to cut him off, a small smile rising to her face. "It was thoughtful of you. Thank you."

He stepped closer, dipping his chin to kiss her softly. "Of course. I don't know how Jared's been tracking you, but he's outgunned. It's probably time we remind him of that."

There was a darkness to his voice that she hadn't seen

223

much of before, and he melted when he saw her concern. "I'm sorry, I wasn't trying to frighten you. I'm just not going to let this asshole get away with hurting you or burning down your mom's place. "

"I know," she said, resting her head against his chest. "Have you heard from Denver?"

"He's on his way here."

"What if we can't find any evidence that he was the one who torched the house?"

"I'll handle it," Christopher said, mouth in a straight, grim line.

"As in—"

"I'll place the fucking matches in his hand if I must."

Maybe it should have alarmed her, but she couldn't fault him. There was an intensity to him for the people he loved, and she felt the same way. There really was no telling what she'd do or say to Jared if she came face to face with him after what he'd done to her childhood home. And it could have been so much worse. She'd been forcing herself not to think about what would have happened if her mom wasn't out of town. Had Jared known? Was murder where he drew the line?

"All this for a story," Christopher muttered and she sighed.

"It's greed, pure and simple. You probably wouldn't know this because you already have money—but do you know how much exclusive paparazzi photos of you sometimes sell for? Whatever figure you have in your head, double it, or triple it if it's compromising."

"You've dealt with that kind of thing for me?"

"I'm your assistant." She laughed without humor. "So it's not just a story. He's planning on selling those pictures to the highest bidder. Trust me, magazines, news stations... they'll all queue up to pay."

"Did you, ah, ever come across... compromising photos of me?"

A blush worked its way across her cheeks. "Not really."

"But?"

"They did once get a snap of you in California. You were visiting relatives or something."

"Okay," he said, raising an eyebrow.

"You were, um, in the ocean? Or, I guess, getting out of it."

"I think I'm failing to see the compromising part."

"Your swim shorts were nearly see-through. The bulge was... impressive."

He went silent for a moment before bursting out into laughter that she couldn't help but echo.

"No wonder you had a crush on me for so long." He licked his lips and smirked. "Liked what you saw, huh?"

A knock on the front door thankfully interrupted his teasing, and Ali was both relieved and anxious to see Denver on the other side.

He gave her a nod and smile before his face turned serious. Christopher led them into the kitchen and Denver relaxed into his seat at the rustic wooden dining table. With the well-fitted sweater and jeans combo he had on, he looked more like a model ready for a photo shoot than a tech whizz.

"Thanks for coming, man. We really appreciate it."

"Of course." He glanced between them, his lip twitching but deciding not to comment on her still-wet hair or the shirt that Christopher had forgotten he was buttoning about halfway up. "I have good news and bad news."

"Okay," she said, twisting her hands together until Christopher stopped her by taking one in his.

"So the good news is that I was able to find some security footage on your mom's street of Jared moments after the blaze."

Her shoulders slumped in relief. *Gotcha, you son of a bitch.*

"The bad news," Denver continued, "is I passed this info on to a buddy at the CYPD I trust and they went to Jared's place. He's definitely cleared out of there. But they've issued a warrant and are checking traffic cams now. He might have had a few friends on the force but there's no hiding arson."

"So really we're no better now than before," Christopher said, standing with a sigh and pacing the floor.

"They actually did have one idea," Denver said, glancing between them."But I told them I wasn't sure if you'd be game for it."

"I'm open to trying anything," she said quickly and Christopher nodded.

"We need to draw him out."

Wasn't that what the cops were for?

"It might be dangerous," he continued,"and I don't know if you're done with the ruse by now." He flicked a glance between them and their linked hands. "Or maybe not."

Christopher rolled his eyes. "What exactly are you suggesting, Den?"

"I'm suggesting it looks like you two are fuc—"

"About the plan," Christopher clarified and she snorted.

"Right. They think you should go to the wedding together and convince Jared to meet you there. Then they can work with the force in Napa to pick him up."

"Just like that," she said dryly and he shrugged.

"Basically."

"I can't imagine Rose will be thrilled to turn her wedding into a sting operation."

"So we don't tell her," Denver said, shrugging and then snorted when she and Christopher shot him identical looks of doubt.

"You don't think she'll catch on when they arrest Jared?"

"Always better to ask for forgiveness than permission, in my opinion."

"That explains a lot," Christopher said dryly. "Did I tell you that he tried to throw Blake a bachelor party?"

"Isn't that... standard?"

"Only if you're classless, darling," Denver said in what was clearly supposed to be an imitation of Rose.

"Bachelor parties are for people who are sad to be getting married, apparently." Christopher shrugged. "That's why they just did one big engagement party."

"I think that's a little harsh," she said with a snort.

"When I get married, I'll definitely be having a bachelorette party," she said warningly to Christopher and then blushed when he folded his arms and tilted his head, amusement dancing in his eyes.

"Wow, things really have progressed since the last time I saw you both."

"I liked you more when you were less chatty," she shot at Denver and Christopher laughed.

"I think we're getting off track," Denver said, narrowing his eyes on her.

She sighed. "I'm just not sure it will work. Jared was pissed after the engagement party, that's *why* he burned my mom's place to the ground. I don't know if he'll still trust me to get this done for him."

They fell silent as they mused over her words until Denver squinted into the distance like he was thinking really hard. "So maybe you don't have to invite him."

"What?"

"You said he keeps somehow following you, right? Pass me your phone."

She dug it out of her pocket and handed it over, shooting a quizzical look at Christopher which he returned with a shrug. "What is it?"

Denver winced. "I'm guessing you didn't know that you're sharing your location with him on here?"

"*What?*" Fuck. Of course that was how he was following her, she should have thought to check her cell sooner—she had never been worried about leaving him alone with it when they were together. God knows what else he might have done on there.

"I'm sorry," she said to Christopher. "I led him right to you."

"Hey," he said, pulling her close and tucking her under his arm. "It's okay. Denver can up the security here for us, if Jared takes a single step onto the property we'll know about it."

She blew out a breath and nodded as she looked back to Denver and he passed her phone back. "So, what? I just pretend I don't know he's keeping track of me and lead him straight to the wedding?"

"Exactly," Denver said, leaning against the wall and crossing his legs at the ankles in front of him. "So what do you say? Feel like being bait?"

Chapter Twenty-Five

I n the end, they'd agreed to Denver's plan because there weren't many other options other than betraying David and Rose's trust.

It was so quiet where Christopher's house was that it was almost unnerving. She could hear her thoughts a little too clearly without the roar of traffic and city life acting like white noise.

Christopher stepped out onto his back porch and wrapped a blanket around her shoulders as she turned to smile at him. He didn't have a garden in the traditional sense, but the enclosed porch overlooked the wooded area behind and surrounding the house. Despite being out in the open, it felt like they were completely alone in the world.

"Are you okay with this?" he asked and she shrugged.

"I kind of have to be."

"No, we can find another way or we can wait for the cops to catch him."

She nearly wanted to laugh, because otherwise she might cry. When had this become her life? Discussing whether to talk to the cops again or act like an amateur sleuth to lure her ex out of hiding?

The air was fresh and she breathed in deep as she mulled over what he was saying. "I think Denver's right. The wedding is probably our best shot."

He nudged her playfully before wrapping his arms around her above the blanket. "Sounds like you're going to need another dress then," he teased.

"I don't think I can ever go back into that store." She laughed. "That saleswoman definitely knew what we were up to."

"You weren't exactly quiet," he said and she could feel his smirk against the back of her head.

"Yep, well, I have you to thank for that,"

He chuckled. "True. Although, it's funny really."

"What is?"

He leaned down to speak close to her ear. "You saying you couldn't go back there... because I'm pretty sure the fact that we were in public turned you on almost as much as me."

Her breath caught a little as he tugged on her earlobe with his teeth. "You're wrong."

"Do you want to bet?" he said and the dark seduction in his voice made it clear that this could be a dangerous game indeed. "Because I think I could fuck you right here and you would cream for me in minutes."

Her nipples tightened beneath the blanket and she shifted on her feet. "That's ridiculous."

A cool hand slid beneath the blanket from behind and curled around her front, hugging her waist innocently. "Oh? Is it?"

His hand slid past the drawstring on her sweatpants and closed over her pussy, pressing his fingers against her before withdrawing to show her the way they glistened in the light.

"If it's so ridiculous," he said between kisses to her throat, "then why are you dripping for me right now?"

"Coincidence," she said breathily when his hand closed over her breast and began squeezing before dipping lower again. Her legs moved slightly further apart as the pad of his index finger stroked her clit.

"I don't believe you," he said and then spun her around, his mouth devouring hers as he backed her against the railing. "Shall I fuck you right here? Or would you prefer my mouth?"

"Christopher," she said, unsure if it was a plea or admonishment as he kept the blanket around her shoulders but tugged her sweats down. "Did Denver set up the new security system?"

He pressed a kiss to her neck. "Yes. You're safe here, I promise." She nodded and finally let herself relax. "Put your hands on the railing, Ali," he said as he spun her around to look out at the trees once more. He ripped the blanket away and she shivered in the air before his warmth pressed against her, and he pushed a hand against the center of her back to bend her forward.

"Are you ready for me?" He nudged at her wetness and they both gasped. Maybe she couldn't admit it to him, but there was something sexy about him taking her here, or wherever he wanted. To be in public and yet alone...

He filled her in one long thrust and her cry echoed into the trees as his hips pumped rhythmically, hitting exactly the right angle to make her back arch and her hips rock into his.

"Do you want to admit to me that this turns you on?" he said when she cried out for him again.

"No," she said stubbornly, just to see what he would do.

"I think I can torture it out of you," he said and she could hear the smirk in his voice when he pulled almost all the way out of her and dropped the blankets from around their shoulders. He thrust into her in one hard stroke, baring her to the air as he stopped again before repeating the motion until she wanted to cry in frustration.

"How about now?" he said as he switched to quick, shallow thrusts and his breath left him in a gasp as he started to lose control. "On second thought, maybe it doesn't matter."

She groaned her agreement and pressed herself back against him as they moved frantically, need and pleasure driving them into a fever pitch until they were spent.

"No, but seriously," he said a moment later, trying to catch his breath. "Do you need another dress?"

She laughed, slightly winded as he pulled the blanket back over them. "Actually, yes. But you don't need to get me another one."

"It would honestly be my greatest pleasure to spoil you," he mumbled as he kissed her cheek and she grinned.

"Really?" she teased. "I can think of plenty of other ways to bring you great pleasure."

He chuckled and they stayed out in the cool air until their noses were like ice and her phone buzzed with an incoming call. Freya.

She winced, already imagining what her friends' reactions were going to be to what they'd planned to do next.

"What's the plan for the wedding?" she asked when she had her breath back and Christopher raised an eyebrow as he re-wrapped her up in the blanket.

"Could you be more specific?"

"How are we getting there? Where are we staying?"

"We'll fly in with Blake, Rose, Maia and Denver."

"Flying private," she mused.

He shrugged, watching her carefully. "Is that okay?"

"Sure, I've just never done it before."

"Well, hopefully you like it. And we're staying in the villa where the ceremony is being

held. My room should be big enough for the two of us."

"Sounds good," she said, nerves starting to stir in her stomach even though she still

had a little over a week until the wedding. "If it's okay with you, I want to go and check out my mom's place and see how bad the damage is."

"Of course. Can I come with you?" His voice was soft and when the anxiety inside her relaxed she realized how much she'd been hoping he would say that.

"Yes, please." She cleared her throat, hoping to ease

some of the tension that had fallen over them, hanging in the atmosphere. "So, is there anything I need to know about the wedding? Any exes attending?"

"Probably," he said with a low chuckle that made her stomach swoop. "I think my parents will be there too, but it's hard to know for sure. I can never keep up with wherever they're traveling now."

"Do you miss them?" She'd grown so close to her mom she couldn't imagine not even knowing what country she was in. That didn't even touch on how strange it felt not to be able to call up her dad whenever she wanted, or that she didn't need to buy him a birthday gift any more. It was the small things that still took her aback.

"A little." He shrugged and gave a small laugh without much humor. "I'm kind of used to it."

"I'm sorry."

"It's okay," he said, smiling slightly. "I made my own family. That's what Blake is to me—more of a brother than a friend."

"He'll forgive you, you know."

Christopher nodded, his eyes going far away as he looked out at the trees. "I know."

Chapter Twenty-Six

Other than the one time he'd been arrested, Ali had to admit that she quite liked being driven about by Christopher. Something about it felt luxurious, like he was taking care of her.

The traffic was awful so the drive to her mom's house took a lot longer than it should have, but she didn't mind too much—it meant she had more time to prepare for seeing the destruction of the home she'd grown up in. Plus, Christopher had a fascinating playlist with a surprising amount of Charlie Puth and she was enjoying this insight into his tastes.

"I wouldn't have taken you for a pop guy," she mused as Dua Lipa queued up.

"Not manly enough?" he teased. "What were you imagining?"

She hummed in thought before trying to hide a grin. "Definitely punk rock."

He laughed, and she was glad for the distraction as they grew closer to the turning that led to her mom's place.

The scent of smoke was still heavy in the air as they slowed to park. Christopher didn't even need to ask which house was her mom's—it was still slightly smoking, and the exterior had two blown-out windows as well as blatant fire damage.

"Fuck," Christopher said and she couldn't help but agree.

"Bastard," she whispered and as soon as the car stopped she got out for a closer look. Hazard tape was strung up, marking the house as unsafe to go inside. Ali got as close as she dared, nose wrinkled against the smell of burning and ash.

According to her mom, the firemen had reported that they'd found an accelerant at the scene spread throughout all of the rooms. It had been deliberate, which Ali already knew, but they caught it in time for most of the damage to be aesthetic rather than structural.

The bay window that looked into the living room had cracked and shattered in some places, and she didn't even realize she was shaking as she peered in until Christopher wrapped his arms around her. This wasn't fear or adrenaline though, no. This was *anger*.

How could that bastard have pretended to love her and then do *this*?

So many memories, burned away carelessly. Her mom was safe though, and that was what mattered.

"Are you okay?"

"I want to string Jared up by his balls," she growled out

and then tried to release a deep breath in an effort to calm down.

"That's... graphic?"

"He deserves it."

"No arguments here," Christopher said, tucking his chin on top of her head. "Do you think your mom will repair it? Or just sell?"

"I don't know," she murmured, hadn't even thought about it. "Everything that made this place special has kind of been ruined now, to an extent. So maybe she'll fix it up and then sell."

"I'm sorry, Ali."

"Thank you."

She turned away from the window with a sigh, not wanting to look at the destruction any longer. "Let's just get out of here."

"Are you sure?"

"Yeah. I'm sorry, I know we drove all this way. I just didn't expect it to be as bad as this. He didn't just light a match, he tried to raze this place to the ground."

"Well, he failed."

"Not by much," she murmured and shook her head. "What's done is done. I guess I just have to focus on what's important now."

"And what's that?"

She smiled slowly and it felt twisted on her face. "Luring that asshole to Napa."

They walked back to the car and hadn't been driving for very long when Christopher indicated to pull over.

"What are you doing?"

His eyes were focused on the road, but there was a soft expression on his face that she knew was for her. "We're detouring to *Lola's*."

Ali blinked. "That's my favorite coffee place."

"I know."

After the traffic cleared a little, Christopher parked the car a short walk from the coffee house and gestured for her to stay where she was. He was back in under ten minutes with a coffee and bakery bag.

She sniffed and nearly salivated. "Are those cinnamon buns?"

"Yep. And a latte with oat milk."

"You're incredible," she murmured, taking a sip and groaning. When he started the car and turned in the wrong direction for his place she frowned. "Are these break-up buns?" Wait. Were they even *together* enough to make them break-up buns?

He snorted. "No."

"Then why aren't we going to your place?"

"Because I've had half a dozen texts from Freya and Jesse since you've been gone and, by the way, I have no idea how they got my number which is more than a little unnerving. They're worried about you, so I'm taking you home and then I'll come back for you later."

She swallowed hard. "Thank you."

"Anytime. Anything, for you."

Her cheeks felt hot and she knew she was probably a thousand shades of red at that moment. They pulled up outside of her apartment and he handed her the cinnamon buns and coffee through his window before kissing her goodbye.

She headed inside and the familiarity of her surroundings made her shoulders relax as she took the stairs up and into the apartment she shared with her friends.

It smelled like cakes, a sure sign that Freya was stressed if she was baking.

Her keys jingled slightly as she closed the door behind her and Freya and Jesse's heads immediately popped up like cocker spaniels greeting their owner at the door and Ali couldn't hold in her laughter, even as it turned into body-wracking sobs.

Their arms came around her, squishing the cinnamon buns to her chest, and they held her until the tears started to slow.

"Been a day, huh," Jesse murmured and Ali nodded, not quite able to talk yet without bursting into more tears. "Are those cinnamon buns?"

She laughed wetly and the bag crackled as they squeezed her harder between them.

Chapter Twenty-Seven

Freya let out a whistle as Ali stood for her friends, showing them the dress and Freya's handiwork with her hair and makeup.

"I'm so jealous," Freya said, eyeing the dress Christopher had tailored and rush-delivered as promised. It was a shimmery gold that worked with her freckled skin rather than washing it out, and wrapped around her in an off-the-shoulder V of layers that almost floated.

"Seriously," Jesse said as she stood. "Boy did good."

Ali snorted, even though she was right. Christopher *had* done beyond good with the dress. She felt like a flame with her red hair and golden dress. "I'm kind of scared to wear it in case I ruin it, and this is just for the rehearsal. God forbid I wear the same dress for the ceremony too."

"Something that beautiful shouldn't be left in a closet," Freya scolded and Ali laughed.

"Very true."

"Are you nervous?"

Surprisingly, she wasn't. Unlike the engagement party, she was there with Christopher for *real* and, admittedly, the dress did wild things for her confidence. "No," she settled on. "Not anymore."

Her friends smiled up at her and it felt strange but right, seeing them sitting on the bed in Christopher's spare room. Like they fitted in there in the same way she did.

"Has he seen it yet?" Jesse asked with a quirk of her eyebrows.

"No." She tugged on the end of her loose, beachy waves and dropped her hand immediately when Freya looked likely to murder her. "He'll be seeing it for the first time when we head downstairs."

Jesse clapped. "I was so hoping you'd say that." They looked at her questioningly and she smirked. "Last time you wore a knockout dress he closed down an entire store to eat you out. I'm just curious how he'll react to this one."

She rolled her eyes but stood and opened the door. "Well, let's go find out then."

It had been weird at first, staying with Christopher while her friends were back at their apartment, but they had visited a couple of times during the week and even though she'd missed them, she'd kind of enjoyed being there with Christopher.

They walked down the stairs to where their luggage was already packed. It was a short drive to the airport, where the private charter plane had been commissioned to take them directly to Napa before the rehearsal dinner that evening. They were meeting Rose, David and Maia, Rose's best friend, there.

Ali had let Jared know that they would be leaving that day and she would meet him as soon as she had the photos he wanted in exchange for the physical copy of her video. He'd agreed, and she'd tried to put him out of her mind after updating Denver.

Christopher waited at the bottom of the stairs with Denver's now-familiar figure. Christopher's back was to her but he turned when Denver spotted her and nudged him.

His face went slack and she knew she was blushing but for once, she didn't care. She felt beautiful. His eyes were wide and his lips parted and even Denver was looking at him in surprise when Christopher continued to gape as she came to a stop in front of him.

"Hi," she said, slightly breathless as he swallowed hard and ran his eyes over her legs, up over the cleavage she had on display, to her mouth. He didn't say a word the entire time, and when he stepped forward she didn't care about ruining her makeup as he crushed his mouth to hers.

"Hi," he said when he pulled away, eyes alight. "You look amazing."

"Thank you," she said. "So do you. You look nice as well, Denver." He gave her a wry grin and she tried not to laugh. "Are we ready to go?"

They grabbed the bags and put them in the car before she turned to hug Freya and Jesse goodbye.

"Hope you have the best time," Freya whispered as she let go and Ali smiled.

"Kick Jared in the balls for me," Jesse said cheerfully as she smacked a kiss onto her cheek.

"Love you both," she called as she climbed into the car and Christopher closed her door. They were still waving as they pulled out of the drive and headed to the airport.

DAVID AND ROSE were already on the plane by the time they arrived and Maia emerged from the bathroom on board as they took their seats.

"You know, I've never flown privately before," she remarked as she swung her legs in awe of the space.

"We can tell," Denver said with a roll of his eyes.

"Don't be a snob, Den," she chided and they continued taunting one another as they began their ascent. "Christopher? What's wrong?"

"He hates flying," Denver said, a little too gleefully as Ali narrowed her eyes at him and Christopher stood abruptly and made a beeline for the bathroom. David snorted but Rose looked sympathetic.

"I'm the same on boats," she said by way of explanation and Ali nodded as they all winced at the sounds emerging from the bathroom.

"Nothing says romantic Napa getaway like vomit, huh?" Denver raised an eyebrow at her and they all grimaced again as they heard Christopher retch.

"Should I go and check on him?"

David shook his head. "Let him get it all out. He'll come back when it's safe."

Denver snorted and they all ignored him as Rose turned to her and raised a bottle.

"Champagne?"

"God, yes."

By the time Christopher returned to his seat, they'd polished off two entire bottles and were making their way through a third. "Feeling better?"

"Yes, thanks. It's only really takeoff that gets me."

Ali patted his arm sloppily. "Well, we're already off so you should be fine," she slurred and Denver smirked. She leaned in close to Christopher and whispered, "Do you think the cops will shoot Jared?" Denver and Christopher shot her identical baffled looks until she shrugged. "Jesse asked me to hit him in the balls for her but like, is it a bit too harsh to do that if he gets shot?"

"He did burn your mom's house down," Denver pointed out and she nodded.

"Good point."

Christopher seemed content to watch them banter, their questions getting more and more ridiculous until finally he decided to confiscate what was left of the champagne.

"If you guys don't ease off we'll be carrying you out of the plane," he teased and David nodded as Rose and Maia giggled together in the corner.

"Oh god. You're right. What if I puke on the bride?" Ali blurted and Rose laughed harder.

Christopher cringed. "I really, really, wouldn't recommend it."

Ali hummed in response, focusing on the rolling landscapes passing out of her window as the plane began its descent. "Is Napa nice?"

Denver shrugged. "Chris would know better than me. Isn't this where your parents live?"

Christopher smiled as he covered her hand with his. "Napa's beautiful. As for my parents, I honestly couldn't say. They do have a place here but they travel a lot now that they're retired."

"Must be nice," she said softly and he squeezed her hand. "I went to Texas once. That's about it."

"Why did you go to Texas?" Denver leaned forward as if the answer was important and she snorted.

"Because Jesse got it into her head that she needed to paint in the desert."

Denver blinked, clearly not expecting that response. "And did she?"

"What?"

"Paint in the desert."

A small smile curved her mouth as she remembered how awful that trip had been and how sunburnt she'd gotten. "It was the first piece she ever sold at auction for five figures."

Jesse still had a small vial of sand left over from that trip that she kept on her shelf in her room, it made Ali smile every time she saw it.

"She's talking about Jesse Cleaver," Maia chipped in, glancing between them all as if to emphasize how cool that was.

"Oh right!" David looked at her with interest. "She did some work for *Horizons* right?"

Ali nodded and then tuned out as he began chatting about art with Maia.

"We'll be landing in approximately ten minutes," the steward said as he stuck his head around the corner to smile at them.

Ten minutes and they would be in Napa. One more day and Jared would be in chains and she would have her life back. She wasn't sure she'd ever been so excited for a wedding.

Chapter Twenty-Eight

Had she said that she was excited for the wedding? She was regretting those words as she was forced to sit through yet another toast to the bride and groom—it wasn't even the real wedding! So she would have to hear these all over again the following night.

The room in the villa that she was sharing with Christopher did kind of make up for the ridiculous speeches though. It was huge, with a canopy bed, smooth cream walls, and hardwood floor. Plus they had a dreamy view of the vineyards from the window.

"Will the food be different tomorrow night? Like, for the real thing," Ali muttered to Christopher and he bit his lip against a smirk.

"It'll all be the same," he replied and she widened her eyes as she worked to maintain her neutral expression.

"Oh, wow, *great*." It wasn't that the food was bad per se, it was more that there wasn't much of it. She felt like she needed a magnifying glass to work out where the food was on the gigantic plates—if they combined her meal tonight with tomorrow's it would still probably be only a quarter of a real dinner.

Christopher's body shook with silent laughter and she wondered if she was still a bit drunk from the champagne on the plane and the wine tasting they'd done when they arrived. She figured it didn't matter too much, everyone was drunk at weddings, right?

The speeches finally over, some music began to play through some speakers—apparently the band wasn't arriving until tomorrow—but wrapped up in Christopher's arms as he slow danced with her, she couldn't say she wasn't having a good time.

"I'm going to go to the bathroom," she murmured into his ear and he nodded, letting her go so she could make her way across the room. The restrooms were ridiculously fancy to the point that she kind of looked forward to needing to pee so that had an excuse to go in there.

She finished washing her hands and tidied up a stray piece of hair that had fallen out of place before heading back out onto the dance floor and freezing.

Christopher held a woman in his arms, dancing and laughing together—and not his fake work laugh either. No, that was genuine joy on his face. And the woman was... stunning. She was tall and so curvy she made Ali feel like a sheet of cardboard. Her tan glowed, or maybe that was just her, and her dark hair and confident movements only made Christopher look more gorgeous than usual.

Ali finally unfroze and took a step towards them,

finally recognizing the woman as a plus-sized influencer that she was sure she'd met once or twice through Freya. Christopher caught sight of Ali over her shoulder and his smile didn't slip. The other woman smiled and Ali saw red when she spotted the hand pressed against Christopher's chest flirtatiously.

She wasn't sure what expression she was wearing, but he finally seemed to notice it and frown a little. So she forced a smile and turned around, picking a guy at random to dance with. Then she took note of him, realizing he looked familiar, and remembered Rose introducing him at *Lola's*, he was her security guard. Nolan? Noah? She wasn't sure.

The song ended and a warm hand closed around her elbow, she assumed it would be Christopher but was surprised to instead find Denver behind her. Her stomach dropped and even though she knew she shouldn't, her eyes sought him out and found him still dancing with the same woman as before.

"I think Noah has work to do, darling. Dance?"

Ah, so his name was Noah. She took Denver's hand and tried to smile. "Sure."

Four songs later, Christopher still seemed to be making the rounds with the unknown woman and she was sat at the bar, getting progressively drunker with Denver.

"Who is she anyway?" she finally asked and Denver laughed like he'd been waiting for her to ask.

"That's Katie, one of Rose's friends."

"Why is he still dancing with her? Like, I guess it's fine

but it's weird he's just left his date to get drunk with the likes of you."

"I'm going to choose to ignore that," he said politely, or slurred was more accurate. At some point he'd lost his suit jacket and his tie was hung crookedly, Ali didn't even want to think about what she looked like right then. Especially not compared to the woman dancing with Christopher.

Ali downed the last of her wine and sighed. "Am I overreacting?"

"Yes," Denver mumbled and she glared. "It's only been twenty minutes."

She sniffed in irritation and thanked the bartender when he refilled her glass. "Fine. But if he's not back here in ten minutes I'm sleeping with you." He choked, sending alcohol flying everywhere and she scowled. "Sleeping in your room, dumbass. I'm not going to fuck you."

"Glad to hear it," a dry voice said from behind her and she raised an eyebrow at Christopher.

"Oh hello, do I know you? It's just that I had a date who looked somewhat like you, but he spent the last twenty minutes all over another woman."

Denver cleared his throat and stood relatively smoothly considering the amount of vodka he'd just tucked away. "I'm just gonna..." He left and Ali turned back to her wine.

"Are you jealous?" There was a note of incredulity in his voice that pissed her off more.

"No, no," she said with a roll of her eyes, "I love it when my... whatever you are, ignores me to rub up against someone else."

To her shock, he started laughing and she could hear her teeth creak from how tightly she clenched her jaw. She downed the glass of pinot and stood to leave.

"Ali," he said and she folded her arms across her chest, annoyed at herself for managing to pick another corker of a boyfriend. "*Ali,*" he said with more exasperation as she carried on walking back to their room.

The villa was mostly on one floor, so their room luckily wasn't too far away and she remained silent the whole way, unable to stop thinking about Katie's hands on his body.

"Will you just talk to me, please?"

She shimmied out of her dress and let it puddle on the floor as she put on her PJs and collected her bag from the floor. "Okay: I'm going to stay with Denver."

"What? Why?"

She stopped in front of the door and spun to glare at him. "Because you ignored me to dance with somebody else and I don't even know if I have the right to be jealous! What are we doing here Christopher? You told me it was real for you too but then tonight—"

"Tonight nothing," he said, running a hand over his stubble. "It was real."

Was. "I see," she said softly. "Well, okay. You know where I'll be."

"Ali, wait!"

She kept going, walking up the corridor and knocking on Denver's door. He opened it with a sigh and a wave towards his couch.

The room was dark and she normally would have

smiled when Denver stubbed his toe and cursed up a storm, but she couldn't find the humor in anything right then.

She liked Christopher. More than liked him. And she'd thought that they were on the same page—he'd told her it was real for him too, but then he'd spent the majority of the night with someone else and didn't seem to see the problem with that. So now she wasn't sure where she stood. Or, rather, where *he* stood.

Unfortunately for her, somewhere along the line she'd fallen for her boss. The issue was that she wasn't sure he loved her back.

"Got scared, huh?" Denver said, surprising her. She had expected he would fall straight back to sleep after letting her in. "Ran away?"

"Maybe," she mumbled and he sighed. Yes, she'd been jealous of Katie but mostly because she'd let Christopher in and now wasn't sure if he was hers to keep.

"Why?"

"I think I love him."

"And that's a bad thing?"

"The last person I loved burned my mom's house down."

"That's understandable," he allowed and a small smile flitted across her face. "But Chris isn't Jared. He's the opposite of Jared. He would burn *his* mom's house down for you."

She reached for her feet and grabbed a cushion, flinging it in the general vicinity of the bed and smirking when she heard Denver's rough exhalation as it landed. "You're fucking drunk."

"So? The point stands. Christopher's been gone for you pretty much as long as he's known you."

"You're exaggerating."

"I'm really, unfortunately, not. It was beyond irritating."

They both fell silent as she contemplated his words.

"You fucked up, huh?"

"Go to sleep, Denver."

"He'll forgive you."

She blinked away the stupid tears that kept trying to fall. She'd been a jealous ass and considering she'd been worried about losing him, pushing him away was absolutely nonsensical. "You think so?"

"Yeah. Especially if you let him eat you out in a shopping mall again."

That time, she threw two pillows. "I'm being serious."

He sighed. "What exactly did you say to him?"

"That I thought what he felt was real. And he said it *was*. Past tense."

"He probably doesn't even know what he said wrong. I guarantee he'll probably come groveling here tomorrow morning. Tell him to bring bagels."

"I don't like bagels."

"*I* do."

"What if he gets hurt?" she suddenly whispered and heard Denver sit up in bed. "What if Jared is more prepared than we thought and he has a gun or something?"

"He doesn't have a license, I checked."

"Yeah, well, pretty sure arson is illegal. That didn't stop him."

"True."

The lamp suddenly blazed on and she groaned, covering her eyes. When they'd finished watering, she found Denver looking at her.

"Christopher can take care of himself. Beyond that, we'll have his back. Plus, this place is crawling with security—he's going to be fine."

She'd surprised herself with the question and couldn't help wondering if that was what had actually caused her mini freak out. Fear.

Wasn't that what Freya had told her before when she'd asked how Christopher looked at her? If there was any doubt in her mind before then there was none now. She'd looked at Christopher tonight and had seen her heart in his palms and it had scared the crap out of her.

A thump at the door made her jump and when the door swung inward Denver swore.

"Okay, well, he came a little earlier than morning but I was still right," Denver called as Christopher scooped her up and threw her over his shoulder, carrying her back to his room.

"Thanks for looking after her," Christopher called over her shoulder to Denver and she squeaked when his hand landed on her ass to hold her in place.

"What are you *doing*?" she squealed as he somehow got their door open with just one hand.

"Bringing you back to our room so I can make you tell

me what the hell that was just now. Then, we're going to have makeup sex."

He threw her down onto the bed and she bounced helplessly as he closed the door and stood in front of her with his arms crossed. It was annoying how she couldn't even be mad at him for carting her around like a caveman —firstly, because she realized she loved him so every time she looked at his face she wanted to do a weird happy dance. Secondly, he was wearing a dark tee and when he'd folded his arms his muscles did interesting things that kept her distracted.

"So?"

She startled, forcing her eyes away from his arms. She wasn't ready to tell him what she'd realized yet. Maybe they'd gone into this too fast. She didn't want to say the wrong thing and make this situation worse. "I didn't like seeing you dancing with Katie."

His eyebrows scrunched together. "So you *are* jealous?"

"I don't know what we are!" She moved so she was sitting cross-legged. "Things have been intense with us since Jared started screwing with us. Are you my boyfriend? Friend with benefits? I have no idea! And then you were dancing with this gorgeous woman and laughing with her and—" Her mouth dropped open. "And you're laughing at me *now*?"

She stood up and stomped over to the door, absolutely done talking.

His laughter cut off as he grabbed her arm and spun

her around, crashing his lips to hers and fuck if her body didn't respond. She groaned and then shoved him away.

"What are you doing?" she wished she'd sounded less breathless just then, but at least he wasn't unaffected either.

"You are... the most infuriating, ridiculous woman I've ever had the pleasure of knowing." Did he think insulting her was earning him brownie points? "Katie asked me to dance with her until her date came back."

Ali folded her arms across her chest, unappeased.

His mouth quirked up like he was trying not to laugh again. "Her *female* date."

She swallowed. "Oh."

"Yeah."

"Well, I still don't know what we are," she said, trying to maintain her anger even as he slowly approached, a desire in his eyes that had her blood pounding through her veins.

"You're mine," he said and the growl in his voice made her breath catch. "I'm yours."

"You are?"

His hand cupped her jaw, framing her face as his lips lingered near hers. "Do you want me to show you how much I'm yours?"

"Yes," she gasped and then his mouth was on hers, devouring and claiming her slowly in a messy clash of tongues and teeth that had her back arching to press her body more firmly against his.

He lifted her easily and she wrapped her legs around

his hips, grinding against him until they were both groaning.

"Bed," he panted and she nodded frantically. He dropped her down onto it and flipped her over, smacking her ass in a way that made her perk it up towards him for more. "No time for playing, Ali. Later."

Her PJ bottoms ended up by her ankles, they didn't even pause for lube but she was wet enough already as he rubbed himself through her dampness and sheathed himself inside of her with one long thrust.

Something about the fact that he was so desperate for her that she was still half-dressed made her clench around him and he hissed out a curse as his hips flexed. A hand landed on either side of hers as he held himself over her and thrust deeply inside of her, the angle so much more than she'd experienced before.

"Fuck, Ali. You're so wet."

"Christopher," she said breathlessly and he responded by fucking her harder until his name was all she could manage to say. She tried to lift to press herself against him and a thrill went through her when he pinned her down to the bed instead, fucking her as he liked. "Yes," she cried out and as she clenched around him again she felt him jerk, coming inside her as her own orgasm swept through her body.

He rolled off of her and she worked to catch her breath.

"Makeup sex, huh," she said, winded and he laughed, equally breathless.

"I meant it, Ali. I'm yours, for as long as you'll have me."

Forever, she thought but didn't say, instead pressing a kiss to his mouth before exhaustion crashed over them both.

Chapter Twenty-Nine

"Do you forgive me?"

"There's nothing to forgive," she said gently the next morning as sunlight streamed in through the windows. She pulled away to look at him, cupping his jaw in her palm and pressing a soft kiss to his mouth. "I was drunk and an idiot and I should have just talked to you."

"I feel like I was a dick to not consider how it would look to you, and then I laughed at you."

"Then I forgive you," she said and this time their kiss was longer, hotter. "Should I show you how much?"

He caught her hands before she could reach for him and shook his head. "Later. Right now, I need to make you feel good. I want to hear you scream my name."

"Cocky," she said, smirking and he tugged down her PJ bottoms, slicking his hand through her wetness.

"Considering you're already wet for me, I think I'm

just being realistic," he teased as he rolled her clit between his fingers.

She palmed his cock through the shorts he had on and raised an eyebrow. "I'm flattered, then."

"Ali." His voice was hoarse and she could see her need reflected on his face. They could take their time later, right now she needed it hard, rough. It was there in his eyes, probably matching hers: fear. They didn't know how things would go down with Jared later, and she didn't want to have any regrets if things went wrong.

Their hands were frantic as they stripped out of their clothes, mouths meeting in a tangle of desperation that answered the call of their bodies. *More.* She wanted more.

His hands seemed to be everywhere, on her breasts, her ass, curling inside of her as they threw off the bed covers. Her back arched and her hips rolled and he pushed inside of her with a moan that she echoed.

He didn't wait for her to adjust to his size before he swung her legs up and perched them on his shoulders as he drove into her hard, their breaths racing as she tried to take more of him and suddenly realized she would never have enough. Not of his taste, his smile, the way he touched her—maybe it was sheer greed but she wanted it all. They were both already too close to the edge and she wondered if it would always be like this for them, coming out of their skins with desire.

Their hips worked in tandem as they reached for the crescendo, his cock twitching inside her as he groaned her name and her kissing away the sound as she followed him off the edge.

The sound of their heavy breathing filled the room as they settled against each other on the bed. "I'm not saying we should fight more often but..."

Christopher chuckled. "We don't need to fight first to do that." She laughed too and then complained when he sat up.

"No... Where are you going?"

"Well I kind of figured you might want to start getting ready. Don't girls like to have hours of prep time?"

Fuck. The wedding. In her blissed-out state, she'd almost forgotten the reason they were there. "Honestly, why do they even have rehearsals? It's like having to go through all of that twice."

"It won't be so bad today," he said, reaching to pull his discarded top back on. "They got the majority of the staring and gossiping out of the way yesterday."

"I'm holding you to that."

He grinned and then reached out a hand to stop her before she could enter their en-suite. "Oh, that reminds me. Wait to do your hair and stuff after you put your dress on."

"Why?"

"I don't want you to yell at me when I mess it all up taking that dress off you before we leave." He smiled slowly when she laughed and pressed a kiss to her mouth.

"Thanks for the heads-up," she said as she strolled into the bathroom still naked, swaying her hips a little more than was strictly necessary.

"I'm nothing if not a gentleman," he called as she closed the door with a laugh.

Chapter Thirty

To be fair to Christopher, she *had* been grateful that she hadn't applied her makeup only to sweat it off moments later after she showed him the dress she would be wearing for the actual wedding. It was probably her favorite of the three he'd bought her. Similar to the one she'd worn to the rehearsal, it was gold but this time a darker shade that bordered on bronze. The silky material was lightweight and clung to her waist but was loose everywhere else. She felt a bit like she was floating when she wore it.

"I was thinking," she said as she leaned against the doorframe of the bathroom and watched him get dressed, his tie loose around his neck.

"Oh?" he asked and then licked his lips when he turned to see her in the dress he'd bought for her. "Do tell," he said huskily as he began to prowl forward, only to freeze when she held up a finger.

"This dress is loose around the bottom."

He cocked one dark eyebrow at her. "So it is."

"Come here, Christopher."

He obeyed, walking forwards until his body towered over hers and her throat bobbed, her nipples hardening beneath her dress.

"Get on your knees," she said silkily and his eyes darkened with heat as he wet his lips with his tongue.

Watching him settle before her had her breaths coming faster with anticipation and when he looked up at her, waiting for his next instructions she knew she might go mad with the power. The *want*.

"Touch yourself," she said and his hand shook a little as he freed the bulge in his pants and pumped his cock from base to tip in one fluid motion. "Does that feel good?"

"Yes," he groaned, repeating the action, and Ali smirked.

"Stop."

A frustrated breath left him but the motions of his hand stilled.

Ali lifted up the hem of her skirt and a gasp that sounded like a moan left him when he saw that she was bare for him. "I want you to taste me. But this time, the dress stays on."

He chuckled and made to stand and walk closer to the opening in her skirts but she shook her head.

"I didn't tell you to get up off your knees, Christopher." His cock twitched at the command in her voice and she knew she was wetter now than ever before because of how much he was getting off on this too. "Crawl to me."

His knees hit the floor once more and this time when he moved to get between her thighs he did so from the ground, looking up at her for approval.

"Good boy," she murmured and he bit down on his bottom lip before ducking beneath her dress fully.

His breath was warm on her thighs and as it ghosted over her clit she couldn't hold back a gasp. Hands pressed to the inside of her legs, widening them, and then his mouth was on her, licking and sucking, wringing cries of pleasure from her as she ground against his face.

"Christopher," she cried and he slid two fingers inside her, crooking them just right until she fell apart for him.

When he emerged from her dress, his cheeks were pink and his mouth was slightly puffy, but it was the glazed look in his eyes that made her ache still. Like he'd experienced something so mind-blowing he'd been thoroughly wrecked by the experience.

Ali backed up so she was against the wall and parted her legs, shivering at the slickness he'd left between her thighs. "Fuck me." It was the only other command she gave and he was unrelenting, desperate in his need for her as her legs came up around his waist and his mouth devoured hers.

They were greedy, trying to touch more, feel more, claim *more*—until his length filled her and drove in so fast they both gasped, dizzy with the sensation.

"More," she mumbled against the skin of his throat as she tasted him.

Christopher fucked her hard, pressing into her with

tight, controlled thrusts that had small whines escaping her throat as she begged for him.

The picture on the wall fell to the floor as the hook finally gave up supporting it and their hips crashed together twice more before pleasure swept them up.

Ali brought her legs back to the ground and they panted together for a second before a chuckle escaped Christopher.

"What's so funny?"

"I think I just figured out why people give themselves hours to get ready." The humor in his eyes made her skin heat as he pressed a kiss to her mouth and she laughed too.

"Want to share the shower this time?"

THE CEREMONY WAS TAKING place outside, which would have been a bold move for early October if they hadn't been in Cali. As it was, the day had been pleasantly warm and she'd even spotted a few people sunbathing by the pool earlier.

Rows of white chairs had been laid out with gardenias and roses intertwined on the edges to make a floral aisle. A wooden arch, strung with more flowers and some twinkly lights, stood at the end of the aisle but still far from the cliff's edge. It was stunning. Most guests had already found their seats, and Ali smiled at Christopher who was standing behind Blake as his best man. They looked ridiculously handsome and even Denver managed to look presentable, though she knew he must have been seriously hungover.

Violins began to play as the wedding procession started and they all stood to watch the three bridesmaids walk down the center of the guests: Maia, Katie, and another woman Ali didn't know but who had David's blue eyes. They wore simple ombre dresses in shades of peach-orange and it somehow managed to flatter all three women as they moved to the side to wait for the bride.

The sun began to descend, and the vineyard was fully cast in a golden-hour glow as Rose appeared from behind a large bush on the arm of what Ali could only assume was her father.

She was beaming, literally glowing with joy as the sparkles set into the lace of her wedding gown caught in the sunlight. Her veil was short and simple, and she had it pinned back from her face so they all saw the moment she laid eyes on the groom—a sort of wonder filling the both of them that made Ali's heart ache in the best way.

Rose's dad gave her hand to David and then took his place in the front. The officiator began speaking and Ali tuned most of the words out as she found her eyes drawn to the man standing behind the groom. Christopher.

In his dark gray suit, it was unfair how handsome he was. It was lucky that Rose clearly only had eyes for David, otherwise the groom would have had some competition on his hands.

A gasp rang out and Ali turned around, a smile breaking across her face as a petite woman with David's eyes walked a chocolate labrador down the aisle, proudly bearing a pink cushion with a ring box on top. His tail wagged happily as people cooed at him and Rose wiped at her eyes as the dog sat down in front of them when David instructed.

The pair exchanged the rings the dog had brought down the aisle and everyone stood when they kissed and the sunset silhouetted them. It was clear that the official wedding photos would be insanely gorgeous.

She met Christopher as he passed her seat and slid her arm through his, pressing a kiss to his cheek for good measure. "Who's the pup?"

"Bailey." Christopher grinned. "Blake got him as a puppy. I'm pretty sure he's the only reason Rose is marrying him," he teased as he walked behind the bride and groom.

"I can't blame her," Ali said as the labrador sniffed at the guests and wagged his tail excitedly. "He's adorable."

They gathered around so the photographer could get some group shots, and she was pleasantly surprised to be included in the photos with Christopher and his friends. It felt like they'd officially accepted her into the group.

By the time the photographer decided they had what they needed, the chairs had been moved so that they surrounded large white tables and a cover had been erected over a makeshift dance floor and buffet table. It was a surprisingly relaxed affair, the tables didn't even have a seating chart, unlike the rehearsal.

They grabbed some food and took a seat at the long table in the back where the bride and groom would also be sitting, only to stand up again a moment later when they re-entered the reception area. Rose had taken the time to change into another gorgeous white dress, but this one was a little more casual and easier for her to move around in.

Everyone cheered as they took their seats and some people drifted about, chatting. Apparently Rose and David had decided to forgo a first dance and people began to filter onto the dance floor as what looked like the same band from the engagement party began to play.

"It's time," Christopher murmured to her and she nodded as she checked her phone.

"Is everyone waiting?"

"Yeah. Denver went to go and check about five minutes ago. You should be good."

She swallowed hard as she ran her eyes over his face. She wasn't memorizing him. Definitely not. "Okay. If I'm not back in ten—"

"I'll come for you," he promised and she nodded, standing up to go and gasping when he tugged her back to him for one more kiss. "Be safe."

"I will."

She didn't know if that was a promise she could keep, especially considering she was turning up to meet Jared empty-handed. She just had to hope that Denver and the cops showed up for her.

How Jared had planned to get onto the site she had no idea, but if he didn't show up to the meet that wasn't her problem. The cops would have to find another way to get him.

She walked out of the main entrance and sat down on the large stone fountain outside, looking back at the villa, the pale pink of the stone stood out even more than usual against the backdrop of the dark sky.

The air was still around her and slightly warm from the earlier sunshine, and it was so quiet that she felt overly aware of the sound of her own breathing.

Footsteps scuffed the cobblestone-style pavement and her head snapped up to see a familiar figure coming towards her.

"Jared."

"Alison." He stepped close enough for her to see the sneer twisting his mouth and the fresh hollows in his cheeks and under his eyes. "Have you got what I asked for?"

"What happened to you?" she whispered and his lips went white as he pressed them together.

"The photos, Alison."

"I have them," she reassured him and then, for reasons she wasn't quite sure of, she touched his arm gently. "Are they really what you want? If you tell me what kind of trouble you're in maybe I could help—"

He smacked her hand away and spat on the floor, shocking her. "I don't need your help. I just need what you promised me. Or this time I'll double-check that your mom is in the house before I light the match."

Dread made bile burn in her throat as she shook her head at him. "I loved you."

"Your mistake."

She reached into her clutch and pretended to rummage around in it, hoping that at any moment they would be surrounded by the cops and Jared quietly apprehended.

Nothing. Not even a whisper of sound aside from the impatient tapping of Jared's foot.

"Stop fucking around, Ali. You can probably fit about three things in that purse. Give me the photos."

She sighed. Where the fuck was Denver? And the cops?

"Oh," she said with mock cheer as she finally let anger and adrenaline take over. "I found them," she sang as she pulled her middle finger out of the clutch and showed it to him. "Dickbag."

His hands curled into fists and her heart started thudding faster as he took a step forward. Ali moved before he could do or say anything else, slamming her knee straight up into his crotch and backing away when he doubled over.

"That's for my mom's house," she hissed and couldn't wait to tell Jesse she'd delivered the nut punching she'd requested.

"Bitch," Jared choked out and lunged for her.

Anytime now guys, she thought sarcastically as he grabbed for her hair and missed, instead raking his nails down her arm.

"You better not give me rabies."

The slap across her face stunned her and she fell to the ground, the rim of the fountain catching her in the stomach and knocking the air out of her for a moment. She looked up slowly, blinking her eyes to will away the blurriness as

Jared dragged her up by the hair. His side pressed against her back and she slammed her elbow into his gut, deciding *to hell with this* as she tried to run from him. This had been a terrible idea from the start. His hand snagged in her hair again and yanked her back towards him, and for some reason all she could think about was that he wouldn't have been able to do that if she'd shaved her head like Jesse.

Ali's foot hooked around his and they both went sprawling in the dirt. Something hit the ground with a thump and her pulse skyrocketed when she realized it was the same disk he'd taunted her with at *Arthur's*. She dove for it and he howled as he realized what she was aiming for. Her heel crashed down on it again and again and Jared fell to the ground, his hysteria making her feel confident it had been the only copy.

He moved quicker than she could have anticipated as he lunged at her, knocking her to the ground as he slammed his fist into her cheek and she felt it throb in response. He raised his hand again—

The blow never landed.

Relief filled her so sharply she could almost taste it. The cops. Finally.

But when she managed to get her eyes to focus, it wasn't to find them surrounded by Denver and the boys in blue. No. *Christopher* had grabbed Jared by the back of his arm and had twisted it viciously judging by the white look of fear on her ex's face.

"I told you what I would do to your hands if you touched the woman I love."

The woman I love. Love.

Jared snarled and attempted to wriggle free, breaking away long enough to clip her across the cheek with a flailing fist as if in defiance of Christopher's words.

A *crack* rang out as Christopher tackled Jared to the ground, his arm now bent at an unnatural angle as Christopher snarled. "I said *don't fucking touch her.*"

There was a loud rustle as a group of men in dark flak jackets arrived and she was pretty sure she slurred when she laughed at them. "Just in time to be absolutely useless, boys. Thanks a bunch."

Denver pulled Christopher away from Jared, who seemed to have passed out from the pain, and a man approached her to shine a light in her eyes.

"You know, that's really fucking annoying."

Denver crouched next to her next. "Jesus. I'm sorry, Ali. Are you okay?"

"Where the hell were you?"

He rubbed the back of his neck and grimaced. "Ah. The front gate didn't want to let them in at first. Not until I called—"

"What the fuck is going on here?"

Ali's eyes slid closed as everyone seemed to freeze. "Please tell me I'm hallucinating," she muttered but looked up and groaned. Partially because it made her head hurt to move her eyes, but mostly because standing in front of them with a face like thunder was Rose and David Blake.

Chapter Thirty-One

"Well?" Rose demanded and Ali was grateful to have semi-consciousness as an excuse not to answer. "Who the hell is this guy?" she said, gesturing to where Jared was being hauled out of the dirt by EMTs. "And what the hell happened to Ali?"

Out of everything that happened, she had to say she was most happy about the fact that Rose had called her by her nickname, like they were friends. She just hoped she hadn't screwed things up between them all with Jared's scheming.

"Um," Ali said as she tried to sit up and swayed, blanching as the world dipped in and out of blackness. "Basically," she retched and then forced her eyes open. "He's my ex- boyfriend and he was just being a collosol-coolaasal—" she frowned, trying to get her mouth to work. "—Big asshole. We tried to tell you but the cops thought Christopher was selling cocaine."

Denver bit his fist as Rose's eyes grew wider. "I know

it's not funny how concussed you are, but it also kind of is, just a little bit."

Christopher scowled but didn't move towards him and she realized he was being restrained by a cop.

"Hey, hey, hey," she slurred, her eyes rolling as she fell back towards the ground. "Lethimgo—he loves me."

"It's good to know that law enforcement is systematically useless at every level," Rose was saying to the closest officer with a voice like sugar when Ali came to. "Just as sloppy as expected. Thank you, sir."

Ali would have laughed if it didn't hurt so much. She wasn't even sure the officer knew he'd just been insulted. Rose crouched next to her, eyes haunted like she was reliving another night like this.

"I'm okay," Ali said gently. "Just a couple of bumps and bruises. I'm sorry if we ruined your day."

"Don't be ridiculous," Rose chided, wrapping the silver blanket tighter around Ali's shoulders. "I heard you got a really good kick in."

"I did," she confirmed and Rose smiled darkly.

"Good for you."

Christopher had been talking with David for the past twenty minutes and Ali was hoping that if he was mad at anyone, it was her and not him.

David clapped him on the back and she let out a breath of relief only to tense further as they approached. "Ali, I'm so sorry that this happened," David said, his brows drawn together as he ran a hand through his dark blonde hair. "If we had known what that guy was asking of you we would have tried to help you guys take care of it."

She blinked. "You're not... mad?"

"Only at myself." He smiled and there was more than a little bitterness there. "I'm sorry that you guys couldn't come to us, and that we didn't notice anything was wrong." Christopher protested and Blake shook his head. "No man, come on. My relationship with Rose is about more than just this one day and we would both rather have known you were safe and happy than have made you feel like you couldn't be honest."

Ali didn't know what to say and it seemed Christopher didn't either.

"I mean, you could have lost your mom in that fire and for what? So we could keep one journalist outside the gate?"

Rose gasped and turned to Ali in concern but she patted her hand. "My mom's okay. She was out of town when the house burned down." She hadn't realized how ridiculous that sentence was until she'd said it. "I'm really glad you're not pissed at us and I would love to talk to you both more about this, but right now I'd really like to go to bed."

Christopher was there in an instant, wrapping his arm around her waist as he helped her stand.

"Of course. Just don't be a stranger, okay?" Rose murmured and she wrapped Ali in a surprising hug as she nodded.

The walk back to their room felt like a blur, and when

they got to the door she realized Christopher had started carrying her at some point. He carefully placed her down on the bed before pulling off the weird-smelling blanket and unzipping her dress.

"I'm sorry," he said, sitting down next to her. "I'm just so fucking sorry Ali."

Her mind was foggy but she was alert enough to grab his wrist when he tried to walk away.

"Stay."

"I let you down. I said I'd protect you—"

"Stay," she sighed and he lay back next to her, fully clothed.

"We'll talk in the morning," he said quietly and she mumbled a reply as she drifted off to sleep.

To HER RELIEF, Christopher was still there when she woke up. His eyes were open and he stared at the ceiling as if it held all the answers in the universe.

"I love you," she said, unable to keep it inside any longer as her eyes roved over the planes of his face.

He pulled his gaze towards her as if he was sure he'd only imagined her lips moving. "What?"

"I love you."

"But—"

"No," she said simply, and he gaped when she pressed a small kiss to his mouth. "I heard you last night, what you told Jared. Unless I was just *super* concussed."

"Ali, you don't have to say it back just because—"

"I've been in love with you for a while," she admitted, "I was just too scared to tell you or let myself feel it."

"And now?" he whispered, something that looked an awful lot like hope crossing his face.

"I love you so damn much."

A smile broke out across his face and she basked in the warmth of it.

"Thank fuck for that."

Epilogue

Christopher handed her a flute of champagne as she sat on the back porch of their house. The air smelled fresh and the trees were still covered in rain drops, but the sky was free of rain clouds for the time being.

She'd only been living there for a month now, but it had felt like forever. They had fit into each other's lives as if they were always meant to be there, like a gap they hadn't known they were waiting to fill.

Freya and Jesse visited plenty and stayed over fairly frequently, but Ali still missed them a lot—it was more of a nostalgic ache though, a fondness for the times they had even as she was grateful to be where she was now.

"You won't believe what she did this afternoon," Christopher grumbled as he tucked her into his side.

"What?" she asked, amused. Apparently he hadn't been kidding when he'd said it was hard to find a good assistant. The girl he'd hired to replace Ali was young and enthusiastic, but also clumsy and a little naive.

"She tripped over the wire she'd plugged into her printer, spilled her coffee all over Denver as he came out of my office, who then knocked into me."

She snorted. "I can picture Den's face now."

"I bet you can't," Christopher said, a smirk tilting his mouth as she raised an eyebrow. He widened his eyes at her and stammered out, "A-ah, no worries at all. My fault anyway."

"*No,*" she gasped in delight. "He's smitten with her?"

"Seems that way." Christopher rolled his eyes. "How was your day?"

"Long, but I spoke to my mom. She's in Germany with Caleb now."

He shook his head. "Hell of a meet-cute."

Ali snorted. "You're telling me."

She had been surprised when her mom had confessed that Caleb and her had got together, but at the same time she was just glad her mom had someone in the same way that she had Christopher.

"Did you tell her the news yet?" he murmured, wrapping his arms around her and resting them on her stomach.

"Yeah, she was happy for me."

"I'm proud of you," he said, kissing her on the cheek and stealing her glass for a sip of her drink. "You've worked so hard for this."

It was true. It had been six months since Jared had been arrested and convicted, and Ali had decided to move out of the PA world and into a new role at a charity for women affected by revenge porn. The pay was awful, but luckily money wasn't something she had to worry about anymore.

She glanced down at the ring on her left hand again and smiled. Her eyes often drifted to the engagement ring Christopher had produced for her last week. It still felt so new, but also so right.

"I love you," she said and he kissed her.

"Tell me again," he whispered and so she did, over and over again until she was covered in kisses and her throat was sore and still, she couldn't get enough.

"Are you guys planning on standing out here the whole time? This is *your* engagement party you know," David said as he poked his head out of the balcony doors to stare at them. A familiar blonde head appeared at his side and Rose grinned when she spotted them.

"So this is where you wandered off to—I think Jesse might be close to punching Denver, just so you know. He's been winding her up all afternoon and I think she's reaching the end of her tether—"

"*Ouch!*" came a deep voice from inside the house, and Rose glanced behind her before turning back to them.

"Ah, never mind! Looks like they've worked it out."

Ali rolled her eyes. "Our friends are like a pack of wild animals."

"You wouldn't have us any other way," Jesse said with a smirk as she pushed her way onto the balcony. "So we're moving the party out here now?"

Christopher snorted and gestured for everyone to head

291

back inside. Ali stepped away too and laughed when he caught her hand and pulled her back to his chest, placing a kiss on her lips that made her smile against his mouth.

"Do you think they'd notice if we left?"

She laughed and tugged him into the house. "I love you."

COMING
WINTER 2024

Acknowledgments

Thank you for reading *Tempt My Heart*! I had a few characters I was attached to after I wrote *In Too Deep* but I wouldn't have pursued this second book in the Living in Cincy world if not for my amazing readers asking to see more. I hope that this book was everything you hoped for and thank you all so much for your support. To keep up to date with my releases, don't forget to follow me on social media, Amazon, and sign up to my newsletter. If you haven't already, make sure you go back and read Rose's story in *In Too Deep*—**carry on to read the first TWO chapters of *In Too Deep* for FREE!**

I'm sending so much love to my fabulous ARC team, as well as the wider bookish community for your support. You are all absolutely amazing! Thanks in advance to the Tantor team who will be producing the audio book of TMH (and my other books).

Big thanks and love to Helena V. Paris, Hannah Kaye, Jenna Weatherwax, Hannah St. James and Sophie Bradley for reading an early draft of this book and helping me shape it into what it now is. You guys rock! Thank you also to Noah Sky for your work copy editing this book, you're a star.

Thank you to Erica from Metamorphosis Lit, without

whom this book wouldn't be making its way to audio. Thanks also to Jess Amy Art for creating some gorgeous character art for my books, you nail it every time.

Lastly, thank you to Connor for your unending support and to my little kitty, Socks, for keeping me company while I write.

About the Author

Jade Church is an avid reader and writer of spicy romance. She loves sweet and swoony love interests who aren't scared to smack your ass and bold female leads. Jade currently lives in the U.K. and spends the majority of her time reading and writing books, as well as binge re-watching *The Vampire Diaries*.

What happens in the dark,
stays in the dark...

Chapter One

Sometimes, Rose really couldn't remember why she was friends with Samantha. She'd arrived back in Cincinnati from New York a few minutes ago and had checked her phone once she'd landed, finding a slew of texts and messages that were mostly from her overexcited mother.

Then there was Samantha.

Rose could almost picture the slight wrinkle between Sam's eyebrows, the way she'd pucker her mouth and nod her head slowly and condescendingly while Rose talked. They'd gone to college together, so she supposed it had been a friendship of convenience, but the truth was that Samantha made Rose feel small. The month she'd spent with Sam in New York had felt a lot longer than four weeks, and as terrible as the thought was, it had only really driven home just how much Rose missed Maia. Sam and Maia, Rose's best friend, had only met a handful of times and couldn't be more different. Where Maia chased love, romance, and adventure, Samantha's biggest ambition in life was to be married with at least three children before the age of thirty-five. While there was nothing wrong with that in itself, the way that Samantha sneered at the thought of doing anything else was more than a little aggravating, especially for someone like Rose whose mother constantly badgered her about 'settling down'.

Rose had only been free of Sam for the duration of the plane ride and she was already pestering her, though thankfully she knew that Sam would likely have forgotten all about her by the time evening rolled around and Samantha remembered all her other snooty, judgy friends. Rose was no stranger to snooty, but Samantha's girl group was on another level.

Deciding to check the messages from Sam and her mom once she was actually off the plane, Rose stepped back onto the tarmac and froze at the well-coiffed woman waiting next to a blacked-out town car, beaming. So much for a peaceful ride home.

"Mother," she said, resuming her walk as she moved towards her. "How did you know what time my flight got in?" Because Rose *definitely* hadn't told her.

"Samantha let me know." Her mom's lips puckered when Rose didn't immediately hug her and she sighed, putting her case down by the car door and letting her mom wrap her into a heavily perfumed embrace. "Though I would rather have heard it from my daughter," she whispered reproachfully in Rose's ear and Rose bit back her sigh. "I take it you haven't seen the messages?"

Rose disentangled herself and pulled open the door with a quick nod to her driver as he stowed her luggage in the trunk. "Gosh, Mom. I landed two seconds ago, so no, I've not checked anything yet." Her irritation rising with every moment that passed, Rose tugged her phone back out of her purse again as her mom climbed in the car.

Sam's latest text message did little to assuage the feeling of irritation. The whole time she'd been in the city Sam had been pestering her about dating. Of course, *Sam* had been seeing a nice, bland, corporate man for the past two years and was certain he was about to pop 'the question' any day. This, naturally, prompted the conversation of 'and who are *you* seeing, Rose?' To which the answer was simple: nobody. She was in the city to work, not to speed date, regardless of how many eligible bachelors Sam had thrust under her nose at surprise lunches or drinks in the evening.

Samantha, much like Rose's mother, felt that Rose needed to 'put herself out there more'. So she didn't do casual sex? It wasn't for everyone! So she hadn't been on a date in... crap, had it really been over a year? Well, that wasn't her fault – dating as a DuLoe was practically impossible between the people more interested in her parents' businesses and money than her and the others who only liked her family name.

Rose was an events coordinator, one in fairly high demand because she didn't strictly *need* to work – so she only took on the projects that genuinely interested her. Take New York for example, she'd been there to organize a masquerade ball that doubled as a fashion show for an upcoming designer. Now *that* was interesting – listening to Samantha ramble about how big her engagement ring would be, on the other hand, was not.

Worse, Sam knew her mother. They'd met at the graduation party her mother had put together for Rose and they had clicked in a way that had been wholly horrifying. If it was just Samantha in the text chain, Rose might have been able to blow off the date Sam had arranged without consulting her. Unfortunately...

Annabel DuLoe: A blind date! Oh how fun, you must bring him by *The Hummingbird*, darling. What a fabulous idea Samantha!

Rose groaned but quickly smothered the sound as her mom gracefully sank into the seat next to her. Dating just didn't excite her anymore, and why did she *need* a man anyway? She was successful, rich, attractive, educated, and well-traveled. What could a man really add to any of that? And bringing him to *The Hummingbird* was just asking for trouble. It was one of the many establishments her family owned and ran, though it was by far the newest, and as such it held her mother's attention a lot more than the chain of hotels she'd bought and renovated several years ago. Going on a blind date was bad enough, but doing it in front of her mother...?

Rose loved her mom, really, but they were very different people.

"So how was your flight? How was New York? It must have been so nice for you to catch up with Samantha. You two don't get to see each other nearly enough."

Rose let her mom ramble on, after all, she didn't pause for breath and clearly wasn't looking for an actual conversation. Instead, she nodded in the right places and made sympathetic sounds whenever there was a slight silence as her attention drifted.

It was only a short drive to the apartment suite at *The Hart* but with traffic and her mother in the seat next to her, she knew this drive could easily double as torture. At the very least, they had the AC.

Her mother's next words caught her drifting attention and she blew out a harsh breath as she tuned back in, wrinkling her nose and hoping she'd misheard.

"I'm sorry, what?"

The frown she gave Rose had her forcing out a polite smile and her mom sniffed as the car finally began to move again. "I *said* don't forget we have dinner with the Blakes next week. Grace has been dying to see you."

A bitter feeling crawled its way up her throat until Rose had to swallow, biting her tongue against her next question because she wasn't sure she wanted the answer.

Back in town for barely any time at all and her mother had already corralled her into dinner with the Blakes as well as this blind date. Grace was her mother's best friend, though their friendship was something of a mystery considering they were polar opposites. If it were just dinner with her, Rose wouldn't have minded too much. But her mother had said *Blakes* – as in, plural. Combined with the fact that her mother was constantly trying to set her up, Rose had an unfortunate suspicion that she knew who else would be at that dinner. David.

Chapter One

David Blake was charming, sexy (if the recent press photos she'd seen were to be believed) and stinking rich. Rose also hated him with pretty much every fiber of her being.

They had been forced together a lot as kids because their families were close and, at first, Rose had always wanted to hang out with Blake and his slightly older group of friends. But naturally she was younger and therefore uncool, yet in the quiet moments she'd resented Blake less – like when he'd snuck her extra dessert, or held her hand all the way home after she'd fallen over into the sea at the beach party her parents had been hosting.

Unfortunately, the unpleasant memories fully outranked any small acts of kindness David Blake had seen fit to send her way. Especially once they both had become older. The dinners and parties and lunches and cocktail meetups had become unbearable, partially due to the fact that Blake had become handsome and knew it and the rest was down to Rose's mother's unabashed hope that Rose and Blake might... date. Of course, eventually Rose had simply begun to decline the invitations. It was for the best really. Blake got under her skin in a way that made it hard for her to keep her mouth shut and her thoughts to herself, he seemed to make it his personal mission to annoy her whenever they saw each other. So far, she'd managed to successfully avoid him for about five years which was no mean feat considering her mother's proclivity for setting them up.

"I've texted you the details," her mom continued when Rose stayed silent. "It'll be nice to have the gang together."

"Will Dad be there?"

"Oh, well, you know how busy your father gets."

She did. In a lot of ways, Rose took after her father more so than her mother. "Of course." Talking to her mom was always hard. At least with her dad, the silences were comfortable. Often with her mother, the silences felt... stifling. Rose was young and accomplished but, somehow without saying anything at all, her mom made her feel like she wasn't enough.

"You didn't have to meet me at the airport," she said at last and her mom shrugged, a slip of white-blonde hair falling free across her cheekbone.

"I wanted to," Annabel said and Rose found herself out of words again. It was ironic really, how alike she and her mother looked. They both had the same slim nose and long blonde hair, but Rose had her father's eyes. If not for them she would look like a carbon-copy of her mother, and when she'd been younger she'd loved that. They'd dressed up in the same costumes at Halloween and done mother-daughter piano duets at Christmas, but at some point Rose had grown up and realized she didn't know who she was. Of course, that was the same feeling most college students had, but it was strange to realize that she'd spent so long being her mother's mini-me that she didn't know who *she* was or what styles *she* liked. Sometimes their relationship was a loss she mourned, despite it still being right there.

The sounds of the city here were so different from New York, more like a comfortable hum of background noise rather than the roar that New York seemed to operate on constantly. By the time they pulled up to *The*

Hart the silence had become permanent and her heartbeat had slowed to a gradual calm.

Rose waved her mother off as she slipped off her seatbelt and leaned in, pressing a kiss to her cheek. "No, no, stay here. The driver will take you wherever you want to go, I'm just going to head inside and relax."

"Don't forget about your date!" her mom called as Rose grabbed her suitcase with a smile of thanks to the driver.

"I wish," she muttered before waving as the car drove away and then headed inside. Luckily, she'd been dropped off right outside the entrance to the hotel because already a few people seemed to have taken note of her arrival. Rose ignored them as she pushed through the doors and into the lobby.

These days she didn't even try to keep up with her social media notifications, but she was certain that now she'd been spotted arriving back into Cincy she would have been tagged in half a dozen photos already. It was a vaguely nauseating feeling, knowing someone was always watching.

Rose only had the small carry-on suitcase to roll up to her suite on the top floor, thankfully. Most of the clothes she'd worn in the city had been one-time pieces that she'd left in the closet at *The Phoenix & The Dove,* one of her family's hotels in New York. For someone like her, re-wearing an outfit was a statement and she didn't feel the need to make it. Instead, the gorgeous dress she'd worn to the masquerade would stay in the private penthouse at the hotel until she ever decided to break it out again. The penthouse was closed to the public – much like the suite at *The Hart* that served as her primary residence.

Her case was a shimmery baby pink color that matched her nails and caught the light as she made her way through the hotel lobby to the elevator, humming idly as it took her up to the penthouse that was accessible only with the special key card she carried.

The suite was a sight for sore eyes. Rose traveled a fair amount for work, planning various events and attending them too, but she couldn't say she always enjoyed it. The travel was stressful even if you were in first class and, while she normally stayed in hotels that her family owned, there was always a sense of the unfamiliar that set her on edge.

Life for a DuLoe was constantly in the limelight and most of the time she didn't mind it so much. Her parents both came from old money and decided to build a business portfolio so large that it was unlikely any of their grandchildren would ever have to work. But Rose, much like her parents, enjoyed it. Having a busy mind suited her, idle hands made her antsy.

But having every move cataloged and analyzed and critiqued came with its own set of anxieties and made keeping secrets and dating a little more difficult, plus god forbid she gained a few pounds or ever went out without make-up – the tabloids would be screaming that she was pregnant or dying. There were definitely a few things about having a high profile that she would change if she could.

The elevator doors opened and the soothing beiges

and baby pinks of her lounge area made her shoulders drop as she took in the familiar gold accents with a small smile. Maia had helped decorate this place to be both luxe and soothing, so it was no surprise that she was in such high demand for her services these days when her interiors came out like this.

A card sat atop the marble countertops, propped up by a wooden fruit bowl that one of the maids had likely replenished for her. The staff at *The Hart* were amazing – of course, it helped that the DuLoes owned the place.

Rose left her suitcase by the elevator doors, nudged off her cream heels and sighed at the feel of the thick cream carpet beneath her toes as she padded her way over to the cream fabric sofa with the card in hand. It had a simple red heart on the front and the paper was thick, likely expensive. Rose smiled softly as she opened it and read the typed message inside. *I missed you.* Maia had likely arrived back home before Rose had and left this for her. The note wasn't signed, but it was exactly the sort of thoughtful thing Rose's sometimes-roommate and always-best-friend would do.

For a moment, Rose just held the note to her chest. She'd missed Maia a lot and above all else, was glad to be home. She was a creature of comfort, that was for sure, and her least favorite part about traveling was living out of a bag and how much it affected her everyday routine. But she was home now and had a couple of hours to unpack and get ready before the date Samantha and her mom had arranged for her later tonight.

Rose looked longingly down the hallway to where she

knew her sinfully large bathtub waited and thought once again that she really needed to gently cut things off with Sam. If not for her, Rose could be enjoying a long soak right now instead of having a quick shower and getting dressed up for a date she didn't even particularly want to go on. Rose could only hope that her date would remain ignorant of who exactly she was, despite going to *The Hummingbird,* otherwise it became impossible to work out whether they liked *her* or her name. To have any possibility of that happening she would need to call the bar while she got dressed and just pray she could get there at a time that her mother was not. Though now her mom knew about the blind date, the chances of that happening were slim. The bar was her mom's baby so she was there most nights, but hopefully luck would be on Rose's side and her date would never have to know he was there with the heir to the DuLoe fortune.

Chapter Two

At first, she'd thought the date had been going surprisingly okay. He'd arrived on time, had dressed-up, and opened her car door for her. A good start. Great, even. She'd tried her best in the car to convince him to go to another restaurant or bar, but there weren't many people who would pass up the chance to go to *The Hummingbird*... including her date. It wasn't an exclusive bar, but it was high-end and often booked out weeks in advance unless, like Rose, you knew the right people.

Uneasily, she'd settled back into the car ride, nodding in the appropriate places as her date spoke to her about his work in the private security sector – not something that Rose really had much expertise in so there wasn't much she could say. This seemed to suit her date just fine though and Rose ignored the unease running through her the closer they came to the bar and the more her date spoke – chances were that this guy shared Sam's views on marriage and kids and a woman's 'place'.

She couldn't climb out of the car fast enough when they arrived, but her eagerness faded as she spotted a familiar dark-blonde head inside. David Blake. Better known as the bed-warmer of most of the women in Cincinnati, he was currently seated at a table with three other women that Rose paid very little attention to as Blake looked up like he could feel her gaze. Rose clenched her jaw and turned away sharply, only to run right into an even bigger disaster as a shockingly tall, blonde woman strode over to her with her arms held wide.

"*Darling!* I'm so glad I caught you. I decided to cover for Lola tonight." Annabel DuLoe patted non-existent stray hairs back into place before pulling her daughter into a bone-crushing hug and Rose wanted to scowl at the theatricality of it all. She knew her mother had likely been lying in wait and had rushed out as soon as she'd spotted them come in.

"Yes, well, I–"

"Your father's upstairs, if you wait just a second, I can go and get him and he can meet this lovely young man!"

Her mom looked like she was seconds away from sprinting towards the office upstairs when her date took her hand in his and pressed a bold kiss to the back. At first Rose was relieved, she didn't need any more spectacle surrounding this car-wreck, but when the guy's lips lingered for too long to really be appropriate Rose wanted to gag and only barely resisted the urge.

"Oh my, what a... gentleman," her mother said at last, retrieving her hand and looking almost sorry that she'd covered for Lola, the Maitre'd who was *supposed* to be greeting her and...Tim? Was that her date's name?

But of course, Cal wouldn't have told her when Rose had called that her mother was covering for Lola – not when it would be more amusing for him to watch Rose rock up with a date and get snared by her mom. Rose shot a narrowed eye look at her cousin and he smirked at her from behind the bar. She couldn't be too annoyed with him really though. With the prospect of Rose's dating life in the mix, there had been no way her mom was going to miss this.

"I'm sure Dad's busy. We're just going to head to the bar." Rose cast a furtive look at her date and held back a groan as Tim (*Tom? Todd?*) stared around with appreciative eyes, clearly aware that not only was he in *the* most up-and-coming bar in Cincinnati, he was on a date with the DuLoe heir. It was something she usually waited until the fourth or fifth date to drop into conversation, though it wasn't often that Rose got to that point as the gossip columns or the paparazzi usually did the honors for her. Plus, she was a workaholic and everyone knew it, more likely to be out for business than pleasure. A dark smile twisted her mouth as she caught a glimpse of David Blake out the corner of her eye again. *He definitely couldn't say the same.*

The last time she'd been within five feet of David Blake was her ill-fated graduation celebration. By this point, Rose had begun to feel that perhaps her and Samantha weren't well suited to a friendship given that Sam had beamed up at her after Rose had walked across the stage and said, "Well, you were bound to do well. Only an idiot could fail Fashion and Events Coordination." But to make matters worse, Sam's eyes had fixed immediately onto Blake once they'd arrived at the party and Blake, man-slut that he was even back then, had obviously noticed. His smile had been big and toothy and Samantha had blushed so hard Rose had wondered if she was having an aneurysm. Sam had been attached to Blake all night, stirring a sense of nausea in Rose's stomach every time she saw Samantha laugh because *ew*, it was *David Blake*.

So Rose had ignored them for most of the night, other than shooting the occasional glare Blake's way, and instead opted to chat with Blake's undeniably cute friend Christopher. She'd actually harbored a small crush on both Chris and Blake when she'd been about eight. Of course, then she grew up and realized Blake was a dick. Case in point, the unfortunate ending of that night – Blake had spouted off some garbage about Rose's taste in classy friends as well as some other things.To be honest, she'd been deep into several glasses of champagne and couldn't remember what specifically he'd said... only her reaction. She'd been absolutely enraged that Blake had hijacked her friend – even if she didn't like her very much – and that Sam had let herself be taken. Then he'd wound her up further and Rose had reached behind her for the crystal bowl full of bright pink punch and assorted fruit before promptly dumping it over his head.

And that had been the last time she'd been in spitting distance of Blake, which was generally how she preferred it.

Wiping her damp palms discreetly on her pale pink slip dress, Rose raised a haughty pale blonde eyebrow when she turned and caught Blake unabashedly staring her way. God, the man had no subtlety. *Three women at his table and he was still looking over here?* Her eyes had no trouble picking him out in the early evening crowd, which was slightly unnerving but was likely just because he was a familiar face.

"Let's head to the bar, Todd."

"Tom."

"Right, yes, sorry."

Tom's arm hooked through her own tightly and she delicately coughed at the overpowering minty aftershave he seemed to have bathed in. Where had Samantha found this guy? Cal smiled politely, but Rose could see the humor in his eyes as he pushed away from the back counter behind the bar and towards them.

"Good to see you, Rose, lots of familiar faces in tonight." His dark eyes shifted to Tom, who was still ogling her mother, and a slight curl of Cal's lip betrayed his disapproval even as he teased her. Callum had also been at her now-infamous graduation party and while he hadn't been around as much when she was a child to see her grow up with Blake, he knew enough stories to know Blake's presence would be riling her up.

She straightened her shoulders and stopped herself from rolling her eyes with a great deal of effort, simply muttering, "Blind date," while Tim remained distracted.

"What can I get you tonight?"

Rose opened her mouth, but before she could say

anything Tim's hand patted her arm and he said, "I can take care of this, honey. She'll have wine, a merlot if you have it. I'll take a beer, easy on the foam." Cal shot her a mocking look and she grit her teeth. Cal knew she couldn't stand red wine and Tad's behavior made her want to throw it straight in his face. She was going to kill Samantha. This date already sucked and they hadn't even made it to dinner yet. She would happily take being called 'uptight' if it meant avoiding painful experiences like this. Tom pulled out one of the dark-wood barstools and steered her into it by the arm, and she wasn't sure if it was because he thought she was incapable or to stop her from running away.

"You know, I'm actually not a big fan of red wine," she said hesitantly and Tom blinked muddy gray-brown eyes at her as he settled into his chair.

"Don't be ridiculous." He smiled at her and she honestly didn't know what to say. "Girls like you love red wine."

Girls like her? What did that even mean?

"Look, Tim, I don't think–"

"Ohmygosh, *Rose!* Is that you?"

She let out a long breath, the voice triggering a slew of happy memories that instinctively made her body relax even as Cal set the red wine down in front of her with a wink. What was it he'd said? *Lots* of familiar faces, god, she'd been so wrapped up in her annoying date and Blake being there that she hadn't even noticed her old college roommate in the crowd.

Rose gratefully spun around and gave a delighted

squeal when she confirmed that it was exactly who she'd thought. "Katie! You're here, oh my god, *how* are you here? I feel like it was forever ago that I saw you at that party." Katie was one of the few people Rose actually missed from college but they both led busy lives, often traveling, and before you knew it, you fell out of touch.

Katie was gorgeous, her deeply tanned skin perfectly off-set her blood-red dress and dark wavy hair and she had more curves than most people knew what to do with. Her piercing crystal-blue eyes shone brilliantly and crinkled at the corners when she laughed, which was often, and Rose was usually one of the people laughing with her. "No! Has it really been that long? Why don't you come and join me? We can catch up."

"I'd love to!" Freezing, she realized she'd forgotten about Tim. "I'm sorry, Tim, but this wasn't working out. Your drink is on me – feel free to have the red too."

Tim spluttered, and Cal coughed to hide a laugh when her date's face turned an unpleasant shade of purple synonymous with the plush velvet stool tops. "I-What? You're leaving? I thought..."

"Mmm... enjoy your night though." Maybe next time he was on a date he wouldn't act like a condescending prick. Life was too short to sit through miserable dates.

Katie gave a low whistle as Rose followed her back to her table, struggling to keep up with Katie's pace in the three-inch silver strappy heels she'd worn. At five-eight, Rose was already relatively tall, but with the heels on she felt downright leggy.

"I see you're still breaking hearts then."

Rose snorted delicately. "He was an ass, and it was only a first date. If he was in-love with anything, it was my name." Katie winced sympathetically but Rose's heart started to thud a little quicker as she realized exactly which table Katie was seated at. No. Surely not. "Besides, you can talk. You look absolutely amazing, I bet every girl in here is dying for your number."

Katie had spent a long time trying to make it in the fashion industry before giving up and moving onto interior design. The fashion industry was not so quick to change – especially when it came to being plus sized. They actually used to see each other a lot at various fashion events before Katie changed careers, and Rose knew Katie still had a big platform in the body positivity community on social media. Whenever they'd done posts together in the past they'd blown up a ridiculous amount – though admittedly not all of the attention had been so good. Despite Katie's undeniable gorgeousness and style, being fat still came with a lot of stigma in the fashion world.

"Rose, this is David Blake, Meredith, and Cara, David's younger sister and my date. Though, I believe you guys are already acquainted?" Katie smiled and extended a perfectly manicured hand to the dark, leather-backed chair she'd seemingly pulled from nowhere. Rose knew Katie wouldn't be smiling if she knew the strange and dramatic history between her and Blake, but there was a time and a place and Rose *definitely* didn't want to go back and sit with Tim again.

Cara slowly stood and looked at Rose from head to toe. She knew exactly what Cara must be seeing, slightly too-flushed cheeks, brown doe eyes that had been coated in a generous layer of mascara, and the blonde hair that had been painstakingly coaxed into heavy, full curls to fall against her cheek. Cara's hair was darker than her brother's, sitting on the edge of brunette, and Rose knew instantly that she and Katie were probably stunning when they entered a room together.

"Delighted to *finally* meet you, my brother's told me so much about you... and Katie has too, of course!" Cara said, pulling her in for an unexpected hug. "Please let me borrow those shoes!" she whispered into her ear and Rose laughed, the friendly welcome not entirely unexpected because of their family's connection. Cara had traveled almost as much as Rose, even attending school abroad, so they hadn't really met at any functions, though she felt almost like she knew her already from all the stories she'd heard.

"The elusive youngest Blake," Rose teased. "I already like you more than your brother." The redheaded woman sitting next to Blake seemed to choke on her drink, but Cara just grinned.

Rose's eyes drifted to Blake as she took in his reaction to her words and fought off a wave of nervousness. A lot had changed in five years. His familiar baby blues were already on her, a slight smile of amusement curving his full mouth as he dragged his eyes up over her legs. His eyes were where Rose's familiarity ended. Sure, she'd seen press photos, but they hadn't really done him justice. David Blake had always been heartbreakingly, annoyingly, gorgeous, but somehow he had become even more so since she'd last seen him – more man than boy and more rugged than beautiful. Blake and his best friend Christopher were just a couple of years older than her at twenty-eight and tended to run in the same social circles. Old money had a way of sticking together. Christopher had always been the nice one. Blake had always been an ass.

Blake brushed dark blonde hair from his eyes and gently reached out and grasped her hand, brushing his lips against it and sending an unexpected and unwanted tingle through her whole body. *No*, she sternly told herself. She would *not* be attracted to David Blake. She knew better. Blake didn't do relationships and *she* didn't find egotistical asshats hot.

"A pleasure as always, princess." His eyes said they knew exactly the sort of reaction he usually elicited, and his smirk said he liked it. Or, more likely, that he liked annoying her. If not for the annoying childhood nickname, she might have even been charmed. Rose couldn't remember if he'd always had this raw magnetism surrounding him, but she was certain she wanted nothing to do with it. Or him. As usual, the only thing David Blake did to her was piss her off. Meredith, presumably Blake's date, was unsurprisingly a little frostier having just watched her date coaxingly accost another woman's hand.

"Yes. A pleasure." Her green eyes said she found Rose anything but, and her thin red lips curled as if she smelt something unpleasant. Rose pulled her hand out of Blake's with a sharp tug. "Well, do sit down, Rose. Tell us, how exactly do you know Katie?"

She ignored the hostile undercurrent to Meredith's

words and gave her a warm smile. "We went to college together, didn't we, Kate? God, I can't believe how long it's been. I actually just got back from an event in New York, so I spent some time with Sam." Katie winced sympathetically and Rose smiled slightly. Katie and Samantha had never really got on. They had very different ideas about what 'made' a woman – plus, Katie was very *very* gay and had no interest in Sam's lectures on how to properly please a man. "How did you and Cara meet?" Fully determined to ignore Blake completely, she was surprised when he chipped in, drawing her gaze back to him.

"Oh, I introduced them, of course. Katie works with me over at *Horizons* now. They met at the staff Christmas party." There was absolutely nothing sexual about his words, and yet he made it seem like they were the only two at the table. His voice dripped honey as his eyes focused absolutely and intensely on her. A bead of sweat slid down her spine at the heat in his gaze and it suddenly became clear to her how this infuriating man had seemingly bedded half the women in Cincinnati.

"Of *course*," Rose said, flustered, reduced to childish taunts in an effort to ignore the way his eyes felt as he watched her.

Katie nodded, clearly not sensing the tension. "Yes, we hit it off straight away! I mean, how could we not? We're ridiculously alike." Katie smiled, clearly infatuated, and by the look in Cara's faded-denim eyes, she was just as in love.

Rose smiled back at her. "I'm glad you're doing well. It's such a small world."

"Well," Katie said, slyly smiling, "not that small. I *had* heard this place was owned by the DuLoes and I hoped I might run into you here. I've been out of the country for a few months on a job for David, but I wanted to catch up now that I'm back."

"I'm flattered." Rose grinned, but her smile dropped as Blake's gaze continued to burn into her and she shot him a glare. "Is there something on my face?"

Blake leaned forward in his chair, a grin edging around his mouth as he brushed his thumb over her lips. "There. Much better."

"I didn't see any–" Meredith frowned, and her words cut-off as Cara pulled her into a conversation with Katie.

Rose's skin tingled where Blake had touched her, and she let all pretenses drop as she glared at him flatly before dismissing him entirely and looking back towards Katie beside her. "Well, we should definitely meet up again. Maybe we could go shopping or something. Cara could join us?"

"Oh! That'd be wonderful," Katie said as Cara squealed her delight. "Do you have to be somewhere right now though? I *did* rescue you from your date after all," she teased, sensing Rose's unspoken hint of immediate absence.

She gave Katie an apologetic smile and nodded towards the bar. "I want to get out of here before my date finds the courage to come over and attempt to retrieve me." Katie laughed as the table all looked to Tim. His eyes were darting between her and Blake, his face pale and his hand clenched around his red wine. "Your tab is on me though. Let me know when's good for you guys to go out." Rose stood and smiled, deliberately not looking Blake's way even as she felt those stupidly-blue eyes on her face.

Katie waved her off, hands flapping in a gracefully theatrical movement that only she could pull off. "Gah, say no more, darling, you'd better run. Lovely seeing you again. I'll be in touch."

Air kisses dotted the air as Cara and Katie said their goodbyes. Meredith remained noticeably frosty and acted as if she were oblivious to the whole fanfare. Rose stood, her chair scraping against the wooden floor, but what made her wince was Blake's words and not the shrill noise. "I'll walk you out."

Before she could protest or shoot Katie so much as a *please help me* look, his hand was on the small of her back and escorting her to the door. Meredith's face was white with fury and Rose couldn't help but feel a little bad for her. Sure, Meredith reeked of knock-off *Chanel* and she had been noticeably bothered by Rose's presence, but her behavior hadn't been entirely undeserved due to Blake's unwanted attention. Cal raised his brows with a taunting quirk to his mouth as she caught his eye on her way out. Damn it. She just knew her mother was going to get wind of this. Annabel DuLoe was absolutely *desperate* for grandbabies ("But *darling*! Think of the tiny outfits and accessories!") and she wasn't above playing matchmaker to fulfill her wish. Her mother would have bona fide kittens *and* probably arrange their marriage before Rose could say so much as *hell no* if she saw them voluntarily together right now.

Rose listened intently for the slightest *click clack* of the tell-tale sound of her mother's approaching heels as they neared the doors. The coast was clear. She all but dragged Blake out the front door, his blue eyes watching her with a wry humor as if he knew exactly what she was hoping to avoid. Well, she supposed he probably would, being one of the city's most elite families came with familiar territory. He probably had to sneak his female companions around all the time to avoid scrutiny. With the ugly thought of Blake's conquests in mind, she quickly stepped out of *The Hummingbird*'s alcove entrance into the warm night air and consequently away from the hand that seemed to burn against the small of her back.

"Thank you for walking me out. I'm not sure why you felt the need, but I'm fine from here." She raised her hand for her driver, giving Blake her most disinterested stare as she did so.

He smirked. "Oh, you're welcome. I mostly figured I should try and be nice to you, seeing as we're going to be working so closely together for the next few weeks."

Her raised arm seemed to turn to lead. "I–*what?*"

That infernal smirk stayed in place as he slowly wet his lips and blinked innocently at her. "Your parents didn't tell you? They've offered your services for a fundraiser I'm hosting, what with our families being so close and all."

Her mother certainly hadn't mentioned *that*. "I–that is, they didn't–"

"Well, I'll happily catch you up," he said disdainfully,

like it was the biggest inconvenience of his life. "I'm throwing a gala on behalf of *Horizons,* most eligible bachelors auction, the proceeds go to charity, of course."

"Of course," she muttered, only slightly sneering.

He raised a cool eyebrow. "If you don't want the job, that's not my problem. It's out of my hands – you know how it is. I don't want this any more than you do."

Drawing her pale pink shawl around her tightly, Rose stuck her chin into the air and glared. She didn't want to work with him at all, but hearing him say he didn't want this either? It rankled her, annoyingly so. He'd caught her off-guard at first, but if he thought she was just going to *sit* and *stay* like a good little girl he had another thing coming. "I got back into Cincy less than twenty-four hours ago, so I'm not all caught up yet. If you're that desperate to work with another planner, then go for it. I've got plenty of people who'd kill to be in your position."

He rolled his eyes and she ground her teeth. "Easy, princess," he said and she breathed slowly, trying to bite her tongue even though he *knew* how much she hated that nickname. He'd first said it to her when she cried about getting the wrong ice cream flavor – she'd been seven and, yes, maybe a bit spoiled, but once Blake saw how much she hated the name, it was all he'd call her. *"When you stop being a brat I'll stop calling you princess, but you're a brat all the time."*

"I see some things don't change. It's all for a good cause and everything has been arranged. Even if I wanted to, I don't have time to find anyone else now. I can tell the next few weeks are going to be... interesting." He paused and there was a look in his eyes she hadn't seen before. Sure, he was a flirt, but he only did it because he knew she hated it. Yet tonight felt different somehow. "I'll have my people send over the details."

Shocked at how quickly this had escalated and not trusting herself to not cuss him out if she opened her mouth, she just glared. The truth was, as much as her mom's meddling irritated her – because it could have been nobody else, Rose was certain her dad had no idea about any of this – *Horizons'* charity galas were legendary. Rose had been out of town for pretty much all of them, and generally she was happy to avoid Blake so she didn't mind. But if doing this would get her mom off her back about this botched date *and* she'd get to not only attend but *run* a *Horizons* benefit...

Blake nodded at her like he could see her thoughts all over her face. "Good. I'm glad we could sort this out. I'll see you tomorrow for our first meeting. Don't be late." He spun around to go back inside, but instead completed the turn and swept her hand into a light kiss that she felt all the way to her toes despite the cheesy move. He gave her a lazy grin before heading back inside and Rose felt queasy, like being at the height of a rollercoaster and waiting for the drop. Working for David Blake? *I'm going to kill my mother.*

Ingram Content Group UK Ltd.
Milton Keynes UK
UKHW040610140623
423390UK00002B/3

9 781916 522015